1

~*Hell's Knights*~

Hell's Knights

Hell's Knights is a work of fiction. All names, characters, places and events portrayed in this book either are from the author's imagination or are used fictitiously. Any similarity to real persons, living or dead, establishments, events, or location is purely coincidental and not intended by the author. Please do not take offence to the content, as it is FICTION.

~*ACKNOWLEDGEMENTS*~

There are so many people I would like to thank; it's quite possible I could take up two pages with it. The support I have received with writing my first book, has been utterly mind blowing. I've had so many kind people offering to help, from blogs, to fans, to people I don't even know. You're all amazing, each and every one of you. Now, to the personal thanks.

To Bec Botefuhr – for tearing my book apart and putting it back together again. She sat with me for hours, helping me put this book together. Without her, it wouldn't be done and she knows it. I freakin' love that girl to the stars!!

To Lola Stark – my snatch grabber. She's my budgie eating, whale toe, crazy friend who kept me smiling throughout this book. Without her, and her hilarious, witty personality, I think I would have given up many times. You're my crazy bitch until the end of time snatch grab, and you know it!

To Sali Benbow-Powers – my crazy, enthusiastic BETA reader. Your notes kept me going, you ripped a smile out of me every time, without a doubt. Your personality is like a breath of fresh air, as I've told you before. You're the kind of girl people go to when they're feeling down, because you're bound to make them smile! You not only told me bits I needed to change in my book, but you gave me a boost and always told me when I was going well. That makes you an amazing BETA. Aunt Sali fixes everything, don't ya know? Best BETA reader ever!

To Kim, Melissa, Jodie and Megan. The group support you ladies gave me was incredible. The notes, the reading, and the enthusiastic message on Facebook - all of it mattered. Thank you all for the time, effort and support you put into me.

To Becky Johnson from Hot Tree Editing, AH, BECKY! You saved my ass. I had no editor, no clue, and you took time out to come and help me. You dropped everything and gave a new author some help when she needed it. Thank you so much for that, you're absolutely amazing and one day, I'll steal you to work with again.

To Ari from Coverit Designs. Girl, you rock my covers. Seriously, you're the best cover artist ever. You just get an idea, and you make it amazing. Without you, this book wouldn't look pretty, which means no one would buy it, so girl, you get half the damn credit!! I love your work!

To Love Between The Sheets for an AMAZING cover reveal tour. You ladies got my name out there, you helped me grow and expand. I can't wait to do a blog tour with you, your energy is addictive!

To Totally Booked, for giving me a chance. You ladies were so friendly, warm and inviting. You shared my teasers and gave me one hell of a Goodreads TBR list! Thanks to you, half of Facebook is now sure to know my name. Rock on and keep doing what you do best!

To Tamara McRae for her fantastic release day tour, that she so kindly did at the last minute. You're a freaking dream. Let's not forget those awesome picture teasers we released each day during the count down. You're awesome lady.

To all the other people who had a say so in my book, be it helping me find blogs, promote, being part of my street team - all of it. You're all amazing, you know who you are. From the bottom of my heart, thank you.

And of course to all my fans – You know without all of you, this wouldn't be possible. So to each and every one of you reading this right now, THANK YOU!! Keep doin' what you do best, and that's reading!!

~*LINKS*~

You can find me on Facebook and Goodreads, some come on down and add me, give me some likes, keep up with my releases, or just drop in to say hi xx

When I figure out Twitter, I'll be on there too. x

FACEBOOK BOTH LIKE AND FRIENDSHIP PAGES - SEARCH - AUTHOR BELLA JEWEL

GOODREADS - SEARCH - BELLA JEWEL

~*BOOKS IN THIS SERIES*~

Hell's Knights - Book One - Cade and Addison's Story.

Heaven's Sinners - Book Two - Spike and Ciara's story - Release date (25th September 2013)

Jackson's story (Late 2013)

~*OTHER SERIES TO BE RELEASED IN 2013*~

The first of an erotic, dark, pirate romance - November 25th

~*PROLOGUE*~

Life isn't easy when you have no one. Everything you do, you have to do alone. There's no one to lean on. There's one to help you out when you're in trouble. There's no one to cry with, and no one to share your laughter. You get tough, not because you want to, but because you have to. Who am I to complain though? What is it they say? Someone always has it harder than you? It's true. It's always true. No matter how bad you have it, someone out there has it worse. Is that a comforting thought? Hell no, but it's a fact, and sometimes fact is all you need.

My family…what can I say? Not a great bunch. My father is some big-ass biker, and he hasn't seen me since I was four. Yes, four. My mother was some pathetic one-night stand of his, at least, that's what I assumed she was because I couldn't see why any man in his right mind would knock her up willingly. She certainly was not mother of the year; she drank a lot as I was growing up and is now dead because of a drug overdose. I'm twenty-one, and while that's certainly old enough to live alone, it's not old enough to survive when you have your mother's debts to clean up, and a crazy pimp after you. I have twenty dollars in my account, that's enough to buy myself a McDonald's meal two nights in a row.

I'm not a bitter person; well, I certainly try not to be. I don't want to walk around with a bitter expression and a bad attitude because my life isn't a picture of happiness. No, I won't do that, because I'm a strong, determined girl. A strong, determined girl sitting on a train that's taking me to a father I don't remember, because he's all I have left. He's also the president of a huge MC club. I imagine he's not overly happy to see me; he certainly didn't sound happy when he found out my mother died. I hate being the child that isn't wanted. It's a shitty feeling to have no one in the world that wants to love you.

Not one, single person.

8

~*CHAPTER 1*~

PAST

She won't wake up, and I know right way that this was a mistake. It was a huge mistake. I grip her shoulders, wrapping my fingers around her arms and shaking. She doesn't move. God, no, this can't be happening. Not now, not here. I shake her again, but her head flops to the side. She has a grey tinge to her skin that I'm sure wasn't there a moment ago. I swallow, feeling the sting of bile as it rises up my throat. I don't cry. My tears are now lodged into a place I can't get to. I stare down at her lifeless body, and I know it's the end for her. Guilt rises in my chest as I force myself to my feet.

I can't be here. I have to get out. I'll call the police, let them know it was a drug overdose. Then I'll be out of here for good. I won't look back. I stare down at the woman that brought me into this world, and I feel nothing. I don't even feel angry that I never got to tell her what I thought about the life she gave me. I don't feel sad that she's no longer around. I don't even feel happy that I don't ever have to live under her shadow again. No, the only thing I feel is a deep emptiness that goes right into my very core and lodges itself there, blocking out any other feelings that may try to rise.

I turn, my fingers tremble as I lift her cell phone and hit the three numbers that will connect me to an ambulance - 911. When they answer, I simply tell them what I know as I stare down at my mother's lifeless form. She's going blue now, an ugly shade of blue that is making my stomach turn. I hang up the phone when the operator tells me to 'hold on, sit tight, we'll be there soon'. I'm sure they will be here soon, to take my mother to a cold place where I know she belongs. They'll be here to free her of her life, but me…I won't be. I won't be here, because now I'm going to free myself of my life, in the only way I know how.

By running.

~*PRESENT*~

I tuck my dark brown hair behind my ears, and lift my sunglasses to stare at the large three-story house, surrounded by barbed wire, that's situated right on the side of the highway. This is the address I was given. Apparently, this is where my father spends most of his time. I see a lineup of shiny Harley Davidson's out the front, all sitting together like they've been perfectly placed. I can hear music booming from the large, red-brick home that looks like it's seen better days. Is that a smashed window? This should be fun. I walk to the gate and rattle it – padlocked – of course it is. I look to my left and see a bundle of old stacked pallets. Grinning, I sling my backpack over my shoulder and saunter over.

When I reach the pallets, I climb on top of them and grip the fence with one hand, using the pole beside it to hoist myself over. I end up in the dust, on my ass, but completely proud of my breaking and entering efforts. After I pull myself to my feet, and dust off the light brown specks of dirt covering my jeans, I walk towards the large house. When I get to the oversized front door, I knock loudly, but nobody answers. Giving up on the house, I walk around the side until I find an old shed that voices are trailing out of. When I get close enough, I see a small door to the left. Taking a deep breath, I walk over and grip the metal handle, opening it.

When I step inside, it takes my eyes a moment to adjust to my surroundings. When I am able to focus more clearly, I turn my gaze to four men sitting around a wooden table. Two are smoking, all are drinking beer. One of the men stands as soon as he lays eyes on me, and I realize as he begins walking towards me, that he's my father. I know because I see myself in his face, and I quickly realize where I got my dark brown hair and sky blue eyes. He's tall and muscular. I'm tiny and petite – that seems to be the only difference between us. His arms are covered in tattoos and his dark hair is

11

tied in a long braid that hangs over his shoulder. He also has a well-groomed goatee covering his top lip and his mouth.

I'm not sure what I expected when I saw my dad again. I don't remember him, so I had no idea what it was I actually thought would come from this moment. I guess knowing he is a biker, I expected a fat, ugly, smelly man with a beer belly. Not the handsome, well-groomed man sauntering towards me. My mother, God bless her trashy heart, had such poor taste in men that I have to wonder how she snagged him. I am sure my mother was once beautiful, but all I remember was the scraggly haired woman with rotting teeth and a foul temper.

"Addison?"

My father's voice is husky, deep and...well...fatherly. I'm pissed at him though, I mean, how can I not be? He never tried to contact me. He never tried to see me. He never made an effort to pull me from the life I was stuck in. I don't know if I can ever forgive him for that. He left me to live in hell. He doesn't know what my life was like, with those men she used to bring home. The dealers, the junkies, the trash off the streets. His life...the biker life...would have been a damned walk in the park. When he stops in front of me, I meet his gaze. For a moment, we just stare at each other, taking each other in, figuring out what we can say.

"Jackson," I say. It's the only thing that comes to mind.

His mouth twitches. Did he really expect I'd call him Dad?

"You look just like your momma," he breathes as he takes me in.

My eyes widen and I feel a pinch deep in my chest. Forcing the feeling away, I cross my arms and snap, "That's an insult, you do know that right?"

He tilts his head to the side, and his gaze narrows. "How so?"

12

I ignore him, I refuse to spell it out for him. Instead, I turn, looking around the large shed. "This is your life, huh? Very…interesting. Where's my room?"

"How'd you get in?" he asks.

I raise my brows at him. "Jumped the fence. My room?"

"This your girl, Jacks?"

I turn to see an older man with a bushy grey beard and steely-colored eyes staring down at me with an almost sexual look on his face, yuck. I give him my best 'if you look at me like that again, I'll punch you' smile, and turn back to my father.

"You jumped the fence?" he says, completely shocked.

"Girl's got guts, jumpin' the fence into a biker's lot," Old grey says.

I spin back around to give him another glare, and that's when I notice him. It's surprising that I missed him, because he's sitting there, looking utterly perfect in his black jeans, black shirt and black leather vest. He has the face of a dark angel. Dark messy hair, green eyes so emerald they're piercing, and a set of lips that, well, are downright kissable. He has a piercing in the lower left corner of his bottom lip as well as two in his ear. I let my gaze travel down his body, thick silver chain around his neck, tattooed arms, thick skull rings on his fingers, and some swanky black boots with silver chains on them. He also has a chain hanging from his jeans. The man likes chains.

"I have to agree with you, Curly," he drawls in a voice so deep and husky, my panties become soaked in seconds thinking about how sexy that voice would sound while he was fucking a girl senseless. "Girl is brave jumpin' into a biker's lot."

I tilt my head to the side and give him a curious look. "Why is that?"

He grins, showing me two perfect dimples in his cheeks. He stands, walking over. I see the patches on his vest now, one that says Vice President and a few other stand out patches that he's earned over the years. I can now see the other man sitting at the table, with his back to me. He has a large patch of a bike surrounded in flames with big, bold letters saying "Hell's Knights". That must be the club name! Very original. When hot stuff stops in front of me, and lets his gaze rake me, I do the same, letting my gaze rake him. What is it about men, that makes them think they can check out a woman openly, but she's expected not to do the same? Well, news flash, this little black duck does not follow rules, in fact, she likes to break all those rules.

"I told you to call me," Jackson says, stepping in front of me and forcing hot stuff to step back.

"Yes, I'm aware of that, Jackson, but I don't need your help."

"Funny that, 'coz you're here and we don't let many girls in our compound, so you must need some help," hot stuff says from behind Jackson.

I step around Jackson and glare at him. "Fine, give me some money, and I'll leave. I certainly have better things to do then stand here with a bunch of scummy bikers."

Hot stuff smirks, crossing his large arms over his chest. "Girls' got an awful big mouth, Jacks, best you put her in her place…"

"In my place?" I growl, crossing my arms too. "What am I? Some sort of dog?"

"If that's what you want to be, sugar, then so be it."

"You mother fucking…"

"Enough!" Jackson yells. "Addison, Cade, enough."

14

Cade, that's his name? Well, it's a sucky name. I turn to Jackson and give him a look.

"Where can I stay, if I can't stay here?"

"You can't stay here, it's the rules. I have a house just down the road. It has four bedrooms, two bathrooms, enough for you to have your own space. I'm hardly there, so it should do you for now."

For now. Why does that tug something deep down inside me?

I shift my backpack and nod. "Where can I find it?"

"Not safe for a girl walkin' round here alone," Cade drawls.

"I can take care of myself," I retort.

"What's a little girl like you gonna do to a big man on a bike if he tries to have a little bump and grind with you?"

"Shut the fuck up, Cade," Jackson growls. Ha! My old man has some fire.

"Can you tell me how to get there, or not?" I say, glaring at Cade.

"Out the gate, to the left, number ten. It's about a five-minute walk," Jackson answers for Cade, thrusting some keys at me and not once moving his eyes from mine.

"Thanks, I'll be on my way. I won't be staying long. I just need to earn some money and then I'll leave."

"You need a job, girly?" Old grey asks.

"Yes, I do."

"We got one goin' at the bar, here at the compound."

"No," Jackson says. "She ain't workin' there."

"Why not?" I say, crossing my arms.

15

"You're too young."

"I'm twenty-one, and last time I checked that is the legal age."

"You don't need to be put in front of a bunch of drunk, dirty old men lookin' for a fuckin' bang."

I raise my brow. "I've dealt with far worse."

"Oh yeah, sugar, like what?" Cade drawls.

I turn towards him. "Like pimps, drug dealers, junkies, and there were always the men that tried to rape me in my sleep because my mother had brought them home for a good time, but she passed out from whatever high she was on, and of course, they weren't leaving until they got what they were promised. You learn real quick how to defend yourself when you're thirteen and a forty-year-old junkie tries to climb into your bed and put his fingers in places his fingers shouldn't be."

"What. The. Fuck?" Jackson snarls.

I turn towards him. "You didn't think my mother raised me in a nice neighborhood with rainbows and lollipops, did you?"

He looks shocked. The big, bad-ass biker looks shocked. "Yeah, I fuckin' did."

"Well, she didn't."

When I glance back at Cade, he's watching me with a look I don't quite understand. Is that...pain? He blinks a few times and the smirk returns.

"I say give her the job, make her put her money where her mouth is."

"No," Jackson snaps.

"Aww, come on boss," Old grey says. "We need a girl."

"She's my daughter."

"Well, least you can keep an eye on her if she's in the compound."

Jackson sighs, and then turns to me. "Fine, we'll give you a run."

"Good," I say walking towards the door. "Later."

"Oh and Addison?" Jackson calls.

I glance over my shoulder at him.

"Ever disrespect me in my club again, I'll punish you. Your Momma might have let you get away with that behavior because she was clearly a worthless piece of shit, but I ain't. Don't fuckin' speak to me like that again."

I tilt my head to the side. "You're a bit late to play daddy now, Jackson. In fact, I am pretty sure you lost that chance the day I turned thirteen and got raped by a man nearly three times my age."

I walk out to the sound of his strangled gasp. I hold my head high though; I have to take care of myself. Feeling means losing, and I can't lose. My mother might have fucked up my life when I was younger, but it doesn't mean I have to live like that forever. I'm free now, and I plan on doing everything I can to fight for the life I know I deserve.

~*CHAPTER 2*~

PAST

"Don't push me away, snake," Jasper hisses in my ear, as he presses my body against the wall.

I can smell his breath; I can taste it in the back of my throat. I want to gag. I want to hurt him, but I am powerless. I have nowhere else to go. I have no one else to turn to. This is my home, and these are the people that are in my life, like it or not. I squirm in Jasper's grip, needing to get away, just for a moment. I know what he wants; he wants to fuck me against the wall. He wants to put his filth all over me. He gets off on taking girls that fight him, so I learned not to fight. Most of the time, he gets bored, others, he does it anyway.

"My mother will be here soon, with her friend for the night. If you're here, what's that going to say about the kind of service you're running?"

He hisses, and I hold my breath, not wanting to smell him a moment longer. His dirty-grey eyes scan my face, and his grey hair wisps around his chin. I don't know why any man would leave their hair so wispy; it's disgusting.

"I might not get hold of you this time, snake, but I will..."

I know he will. He always does. All I've done is buy myself a night, maybe two, if I'm lucky. He'll come back, and perhaps next time, he won't listen to my attempts at turning him away.

"I'm sure you will," I snarl, in a low, dangerous voice.

"You make sure your Momma brings in a good amount tonight. Don't let her pass out on her client again. That no good piece of shit is startin' to get on my nerves."

"Go and find yourself some fresh meat then, and leave us alone," I growl.

He lets me go, and the instant pressure release throughout my body is massive.

"I've got fresh meat. It's you, snake."

"You'll never make me your whore, Jasper."

"But I will, because you know as well as I do that this is your life, like it or not."

"Not."

He smirks, cold, evil, and then turns and walks towards the door. When he gets to it, he digs into his pockets and pulls out a bag of white powder. He tosses it at me, and I catch it in one hand.

"Make sure your Momma don't get that 'till morning. We both know she likes it for breakfast, and from what I hear, so do you. Make sure she keeps her legs open and her eyes wide tonight, got me?"

"Go fuck yourself," I hiss.

"Don't make me turn around, snake, because if I do, you won't like how it ends. Get my money for me tonight, or face what's coming for you. Another week with no food doesn't sound too appealing, now, does it?"

At my expression, and the loud grumble my stomach makes, he chuckles.

"Thought as much, do what I ask, snake."

Then he's gone. Just like that. I stare down at the bag of powder in my hand. Sighing, I open it, line it up on the table, get to my knees, roll up an old five dollar note, and snort it.

He's right, I do need it as much as her.

I need it because it's my only escape.

~*PRESENT*~

I walk down the road after getting out of the compound. I really don't know what I feel right now. I've gone over so many different scenarios in my head. I think about the situation, and what it will all mean for me now that I'm here. Seeing my father again, seeing the horror in his eyes when I told him my story makes me wonder if I've made the right choice. I don't know if he'll ever get used to having me around or if things will just continue to spiral downwards.

Things could be much worse for both of us though, of that I'm sure. I've been around rotten people in my life, mostly pimps, who consider feelings to be worthless emotions that are simply not needed. Cold, heartless people who think hurting another person is okay. That's the difference between these bikers and the pimps I used to live with. Bikers will fight for what they love and believe in…Pimps don't care. They do what they have to do for business and money. I don't think bikers fall completely into that category; at least, I'd like to hope they don't.

Seeing my father's face when I gave him a glimpse at my life, told me that even though he doesn't know me, he would fight for me. That's a nice feeling to have, even if I know it's temporary and I can't hold onto it. I don't belong here. Honestly, right now, I don't know where I belong. How do you fit into any place when you've lived a life protecting yourself and trusting no one? I can't get comfortable anywhere, in fear it will just end badly for me and I'll break the wall I've built so high around myself. At least, for the moment, I know that I'm safe and I have protection. That's all I need for the moment. He can't find me if I'm protected.

As I continue down the road, rocks crunch under my feet as I contemplate my next move. I have no money, and I really don't have any other place to go. This is it for me, this compound, this world, this job - working in a bar with a bunch of bikers I don't know. I have to survive though, even if surviving is hard. I just have to do what I do best, and that is to fight through the next few months and get enough money to figure out where to go from here. Once I am out of this state, hell, out of this country…then maybe I can start piecing my fucked-up life together, tatter by tatter, until it resembles something worth believing in.

When I get to my father's old, run down house, I stare at the massive building for a long moment. It's ugly, like, really ugly, but I've lived in much worse, so to me, it's like a fine hotel. It's tall, two stories, and it's surrounded by a rickety looking deck. I think it was once white, but the paint is now peeling and faded to a dirty brown. I step through the front gate and walk up to the front door. As soon as I unlock it and step inside, I sigh. Typical male home, beer bottles everywhere, clothes, pizza boxes, you name it. It's clear to me, after one glance at the old faded blue kitchen, that the dishes haven't been done for at least three days, and the laundry…don't even get me started on the laundry.

I stare around my new home. It's not great but it's safe. I've been to many places in my life, most of which weren't fit for fleas, let alone people. So I know I can make it work here. I slip my shoes off and walk into the kitchen. I open the fridge, cringe, and close it. My God, what in the hell was that God awful smell? Do I even want to know? Guess I will deal with that one later. I notice along with dishes, laundry and cleaning up, my father also doesn't shop often. Turning on my heel, I walk out into the living room and up the stairs to my left. At the top, I step into a long hallway, with faded wooden floors. I stare around at all the closed doors; I guess I have to open them and find out which room is the spare one. I begin walking down the hall, opening doors as I go. The first to my left is definitely a man's room, so I am guessing my father's considering he's the only man who lives here. At least, I think he is.

The second room is an old bathroom, with cream tiles, a cream shower that needs a damn good clean, and an awful rusted mirror.

The third door is the spare room. I can tell this by the mass of suitcases, pillows, old blankets and other junk that's been so nicely dumped on the queen sized bed. With a sigh, I walk in and get to work clearing it all off. When I've managed to tidy the room up, I take a good look. Green curtains, nice. Wooden floors in here too, though most of the surface is covered with an old, frayed rug. The bed has a squishy, sink into it, kind of mattress. I dispose of the sheets and pillows right away, I will hit my father up for some new ones later on. If not, they're getting washed three times. At least.

When I've freshened up, thrown the sheets into the washing machine and put my clothes into the old wooden dresser, I head downstairs. Time to tackle this kitchen. I spend the next hour cleaning, gagging and cursing my father for being so incredibly lazy. Seriously, the man could at least invest in a dishwasher to save us all some pain. This kitchen is a pigsty, the entire house is a pigsty. I hear the front door open just as I am giving myself a pep talk about tackling the fridge and handling whatever has died in there. I turn, and see Jackson walking in. He stops when he sees me dissecting his kitchen with a scowl. He tosses his helmet down and shrugs off his leather jacket.

"Have you ever heard of doing dishes?" I say, crossing my arms.

He shrugs, giving me a 'who cares' kind of expression. "I do the dishes when I need to do the dishes. I've got better things to do in my life."

I throw him a sarcastic expression. "I couldn't imagine what could possibly be more important than dishes."

I'm pretty sure I see his lips twitch, which surprises me. I imagine that Jackson was a complete looker in his day. In fact, I have no doubt about it. While older now, I don't doubt he still attracts plenty of female attention. He must have had no brains in his head, though, the day he decided my mother was worth a shot. I walk around the kitchen counter, and stop in front of him.

22

"What've you got to eat in this joint?"

He waves a dismissive hand, and drops his ass onto the couch. "You already know I have nothing. I don't cook. I don't shop. That's what take out's for. Plus, I'm at the compound more than I'm here. If you want food, get it yourself. I'm sure you can sort it out."

"Jackson, if you want me to make food and eat, then you should give me some money. Being my father and all..."

He grins at me like that's completely amusing to him. "You wanna be my daughter, you get things the way any daughter does - by working for it. You want money, go and earn it. You want me to buy food, then you do something to make me feel as though you deserve it. It ain't a pretty walk in the park here, princess. Nothin' comes easy, you ought to learn that."

I walk over, feeling my blood boil, feeling my anger getting the better of me. "You think I don't know how to support myself? You think I don't know how to work for what I want? You know I haven't had a beautiful life. Nothing came easily to me, not a single, damned thing. I'll earn every morsel that goes into my mouth, you piece of shit."

Jackson stares at me, completely and utterly confused, and a little stunned. It takes him a moment to get a stony expression back on his face. "I get you had a hard life. I get you have your own back, and you do what you gotta to survive. I get that you're here temporarily, and you don't want to be, but don't think you can come into my house speakin' to me the way you just did. I'll boot you out on your fuckin' ass."

I storm over, throwing my hands on my hips. He shouldn't be getting a reaction like this; it's not worth it, and yet here I am about to explode at the one man that is taking me in. The one man who is likely going to be my only protection. "If you want to speak to me like that, I'll speak to you like that. If you don't want me here, you shouldn't have asked me to stay. I'll find somewhere else, and I'll survive doing it. If you've got such a problem with this," I say indicating myself and the room in general, "then tell me and I'll pack my shit now and leave. I don't need you, as much as you don't fucking need me."

I lunge forward, gripping my backpack, but Jackson is faster. He's up, hand wrapped around my arm before I even get a chance to blink. He pulls me into his face, his eyes are flaring with anger. "Girl," he says in a rough angry tone, "you might be my daughter, and you might have had a tough life, but you ever speak to me like that again, I'll put you on your fuckin' ass."

Swallowing, I force the tears back that well in my eyes. I snatch my arm from Jackson's grip and heave my next words out. "I know you don't want me here. I know you don't like me disrupting your life, but do you think I like it either? Do you think I asked for any of this? You want to put me on my ass? Go right ahead. It's not like it hasn't been done many times before. If you want me out, Jackson, speak up. I'll leave. I'll walk out and find my way, because I always do. Even if it means I find it in the only way I learned how. I'll do what I have to, to survive and protect myself. I'm so incredibly sorry that I was thrown upon you. Perhaps next time you don't want children in your life, you should keep your dick wrapped."

Then I turn and rush up the stairs, just before the hot tears spill out of my eyelids.

~*~*~*~

I hear Jackson moving around downstairs for a while after my outburst. At least he didn't come up and kick me out. I curl up on the old, squishy bed, wrapped in my pajamas, and think about which move I should take next. I really do need to keep my mouth shut, or I'll have no next move. Jackson clearly doesn't take any shit, and maybe that's a good thing, but he needs to understand I don't either. Maybe I inherited it from him. I slip off my bed, curious, wanting to ask the one question that I've been wanting an answer to

24

for such a long time. I don't even know if Jackson will talk to me, but it's worth a shot.

I walk out of my room, treading down the hall quietly. I creep down the stairs and peer into the living room. Jackson is on the couch, pizza in hand, beer in his lap, football on the television. I watch him for a long moment, still in a slight amount of shock that this man is actually my father. I always knew he was a biker. I always knew he had a hard life, but I guess seeing him in front of me is still surreal. I grip the railings on the stairs, and decide I won't move any further down than this, just in case he decides to get snappy at me.

"Why her?"

He turns, looking at me standing on the stairs. His eyes scan me for a moment, before he turns back to the television. I guess he doesn't want to talk to me. I am about to turn, when he says, "Your Momma?"

I stop, swallowing. "Yeah, why her?"

He shrugs. "She was beautiful, sweet, funny, and she caught my eye. I didn't know she had such a fucked up life. She didn't show that to me."

I'm shocked by this. "It wasn't just one night?"

He turns, meeting my gaze. "That what she told you?"

I shake my head. "She told me you were a biker. That was it."

He stares at me, his blue gaze locking me in place. Then he holds up a slice of pizza. "Hungry?"

I nod, daring to step off the last step and walk over. I sit on the couch over from him, and I take a slice of pizza.

"Your Momma never told you how we met? Nothin'?"

I shake my head, biting into my pizza. Jackson watches me again, then he stands, walking off down the hall. I stare blankly at him, confused for a moment, until he returns with an old photo album. He places it down next to me, and then takes his seat on the couch again. I stare down at the tattered, maroon album confused.

"Open it," he says.

I slip the album open, and stare for a long while, at the pictures in front of me. The woman with dark hair, brown eyes and olive skin in front of me is so stunning, I don't recognize her as my mother. She never looked like that, not that I can remember. I run my fingers over the picture. She's laughing in it, standing beside a motorcycle, her hair blowing in the breeze. I swallow, feeling my throat clenching painfully. Slowly, I move my eyes to the next picture. She's pregnant in this picture, her swollen belly clearly noticeable. Jackson is beside her, his hand resting on it, a smile on his face. I was right, he was incredibly good looking. When I get to the next picture, my throat does close over.

It's my mother, Jackson and...well...I guess me. I'm only about a year old, tiny, smiling, happy. I stare at the picture for such a long time. So there was a time in my life, where things were perfect? There was a time when I was just a happy, normal child? I run my fingers over the picture, and then look up at Jackson. He's watching me intently, focusing on my expression, no doubt trying to gauge my reaction. I am in shock. It takes me a moment to splutter out the words swarming around in my head.

"You...she wasn't a one night stand?"

He shakes his head. "No, she wasn't."

"Then, you wanted me?"

His eyes widen, and for a moment he seems too shocked to speak. "Of course I fuckin' wanted you. I wanted that life. I wanted a family."

"Then what went wrong?" I croak out.

"Jasper happened."

I flinch, that name sends shivers up my spine and lodges itself into the coldest parts of my soul. Jasper is, or was, my mother's pimp. He was also my nightmare, and took my virginity before I was ready to give it. He's after me now, for more reasons than one.

"You're familiar with Jasper?" Jackson says.

"Something like that," I say, not wanting to give my father any more information. "My mother was a whore before she met you then?"

He nods, his face scrunching with a moment of pain and a little disgust. "Yeah, she was. I didn't know. I met her at a bar one night, didn't even fuckin' think that she was there whoring. We didn't fuck that night; we talked all night long. We did that for about four or five days, things were good; I liked her. Then we got together one heated night and didn't use protection. She got pregnant and we decided to give it a go. She never even indicated that she had that kind of life. She told me her parents lived overseas, and were wonderful. I didn't even question when she had us movin' around all the time. I now know it was because Jasper was after her. She owed him money. When he caught up with us, you were just about to turn four. I still remember the look on her face when he showed up at our door. When he told me what he was there for, I didn't fuckin' believe him. No way he was tellin' the truth. No way my sweet, loving Emily was a fuckin' whore. I confronted her. She told me it was true, that she was a whore. I lost my shit and walked out; I was hurt and angry. When I came back, she was gone and so were you. Turns out her name wasn't even Emily. I didn't know how to find her. How do you find someone with a false name and a false life?"

I ponder this information for a long moment before answering. "You didn't abandon me like she said?"

27

He looks hurt by that. "No, fuck no. I came back when I cooled down and she was gone. Went with that little prick, never even stayed behind to explain. She took you with her."

"Then the first time you heard about me since then, was after she died?"

"Yeah, apparently she had my name in her will. That's how I got in contact with you. They rang me to tell me she passed on."

"Yeah, they told me your name was in there; it's how we located you."

He nods. "I never intended for you to have the life you did, but I assumed she might have taken you to her wonderful parents, and that she got out of that bad life. She did love you, Addison."

I flinch. "Don't," I whisper. "For starters, her parents are dead. They were never real, and secondly, you don't know what she was like."

"I saw what she was like with you, before she left. You were her sunshine."

"Do you feed your sunshine to the wolves? Do you drag your sunshine through a life so violent and horrible it damages it for life? No you don't. If she loved me, she would have sent me with you. If she loved me, she would have made a decent life for us. She would have found a way."

"Sometimes, there is no way, when you've sunk yourself so deep."

I stare at him, hurt. "You're on her side? You think it's okay what she did?"

"No, I don't fuckin' think it's okay. If she was here, I'd put her on her ass. All I'm sayin' is that sometimes things get so bad, you can't go back."

"You can always go back, Jackson."

I stand before he can say anything else, and begin walking back towards the stairs. I don't want to talk about this anymore, what's the point? He's got his opinion, and I don't need to hear that my mother loved me, when I know she didn't. If some part of her did, it wasn't enough. I am just about at the stairs when Jackson calls my name. I stop and stare back at him, forcing my emotions down.

"For what it's worth, I never wanted to let you go and I'm fuckin' glad you're here."

With that, he flicks the television off, then he disappears into the small study, leaving me completely and utterly speechless.

~*CHAPTER 3*~

PAST

I rub my arms. I'm cold, and I can't stop shaking. I hate coming down, going up is always a relief, coming down sucks. I don't do it often enough to become used to it, even then, I don't think I could. I only do it to escape him. It's all I have. I feel my eyes darting around, even though my body isn't doing anything but shaking. I scan the room; I'm sure I heard something. I scurry towards the curtains and peer out, but there's no one around. I'm sure I hear phone's ringing, but I don't have a phone. I hate this. I hate it. Sweat slides down my face, trickling over my cheeks and down my neck. I shake so violently my teeth clatter together.

"There she is."

I hear the raspy voice that haunts my dreams, and I turn to see Jasper standing at the door, fully naked, stroking his cock. I gag. I gag and gag until I struggle to breathe. I feel so utterly helpless, like no matter what I do right now, I won't escape this. There is no feeling in the world that could be worse than being completely trapped with no way out.

"So nice to see you're excited to see me, as you can see, I'm excited to see you."

Please, just leave me alone. All I want, is to be left alone. I don't want to be touched. I don't want to be forced. I just want freedom. Just for one moment. I will fight. I will beg, but in the end, the result is always the same. He will take what he wants, and he will leave a part of me that much more broken.

"Leave me be," I rasp.

"Coming down from that meth high? Always fun."

I hate him. One day, I'll kill him. I will. I'll take a knife to his heart, or a gun to his head. One day, I'll free myself from this.

"Just. Get. Lost," I wail, and my voice sounds high pitched and childlike.

"Now come on, Addison, you and I both know you enjoy what I do to you."

I gag again, and this time a dribble of bile slides from my throat, out of my mouth, and down my chin. He won't leave, he never does. When he's like this, I can fight as much as I like, but he won't leave. The only thing I can do is survive it. I grip the side of the table, pulling myself closer to it. There's still a line of white powder on the edge. I pull out an old five dollar note and roll it up, then I grip my hair, pulling it away from my face. I press the rolled note into my nose, and I lean down, snorting it until it's burning and my eyes are watering. In a moment, just a small moment, everything will be fuzzy.

That's how I survive. No one said it was right.

~*PRESENT*~

The first day at work in the compound is utterly gut wrenching. Though I try not to show it, I am having a slight breakdown inside. I spent the entire morning in my room, pulling my hair up, fixing my make-up and trying my best to keep my nerves under wraps. I don't know how I'll be treated. I don't know if they'll hate me, or like me, or both. I've had many experiences in my life, but bikers aren't one of them. There's a certain part of their lives that sparks an inner fear inside me. It's the dominant, strong, never back down part, I think. I have to keep my chin up, though, because I know that I can beat anything that's thrown at me. Heck, I have beaten everything that's been thrown at me.

Luckily for me, most of the guys are good when I arrive at work. A few even give me smiles of encouragement. This surprises me. I honestly thought they would give me hell. Maybe they're just being nice because I'm Jackson's daughter. I meet a few of the other girls, or 'old ladies' as most like to call them. The two that are constantly around, Mary and Poppy, seem decent enough. They help me out where I need it, and give me a run down on the club and how it works. They also inform me that I wouldn't be here if it wasn't for the fact that I was Jackson's daughter. Fair enough, I suppose. Rules are rules, and let me tell you, I've been given a fair list of them.

Jackson gave me a run down on the way out of the house this morning. He told me to shut my mouth, do my job and then leave the compound. I wasn't to go snooping, or walking around, or interrupting anyone's day-to-day activity. I was there to work, plain and simple. So, here I am, doing my job, keeping my mouth shut and avoiding all contact with the bikers unless they ask me directly for something, which is usually a beer.

I am mid-way through cleaning some glasses when a cool, smooth, sexy voice fills my ears. My body shivers. It's an automatic reaction to a voice that sounds like his. I lift my eyes to see Cade, the man I met yesterday, leaning over the bar.

"Hello there, sugar, got a beer for me?"

I stare at him for a long moment, then I turn and grip a beer from the fridge, tossing it at him.

"Ain't ya gonna open that for me?"

Smart ass. I turn with a silky smile and uncap the top. He grins at me, showing those devastating dimples. His green eyes look divine under this light, so bright, so clear, anyone would get lost in those eyes.

"How's your first day goin'?" he asks.

I raise my brow at him. "You're not interested in my first day. What is it you really want to ask?"

He grins again, like he's completely amused by every single word that leaves my mouth.

"You got a man?"

Seriously? I put my hands on my hips and shake my head.

"Does that line work on women?"

"I don't have to use lines on women, sugar."

I bet he doesn't.

"Then why the question?"

"Curiosity, see, I know you're runnin' from somethin'. I'm figuring it's a man, but I could be wrong."

"You're wrong, and I'm not running."

He raises a brow. "No?"

"No."

"Think you're fuckin' lyin' now."

I snort. "And you know this because you know me so incredibly well that you can see I'm lying?"

He chuckles. "Sugar, you're lying, I can see it written all over you. The way your eyes twitched when I said that, the way your body stiffened just a touch. So, I assume I'm right about one thing, you're runnin' from somethin'. Not a man, but somethin'."

"My life," I grind out, hating that he is so right, "is none of your fucking business."

"A reaction, you know what that means, yeah?" he teases.

33

"It means if you don't shut up, I'll dive over this bar and give you something to talk about."

He stares at me a long moment, then throws his head back and roars with laughter. My fists clench, I'm so damned angry right now. I want to punch that beautiful jaw. I want to grip his hair and tug until he growls. I just want to hurt him.

"Sugar, you're extremely entertaining, by all means, keep goin'."

I glare at him. "Can you leave? I'm busy."

He looks at the empty bar. "Oh yeah?"

"Fuck off, Cade."

"Ouch, you wound me."

I sigh, giving up on my attempt to get rid of him. I pick up the dish towel and continue drying the glasses. For a long moment, he watches me, just letting his gaze run over my body. I feel every second of it too.

"Where you from?"

I look up at him, brows raised. "None of your business."

"Can't a man even have a conversation with you? Didn't anyone teach you manners, sugar?"

I narrow my eyes at him. "Where are you from?" I throw back.

He smirks, "I'm from here, now it's your turn."

I roll my eyes at him. "I'm not telling you where I'm from."

"Running from something?"

"Are we back to that again?" I say, placing the glass down and picking up another one.

"Well, tell me where you're from and we won't be back to that."

"No."

"Fine, tell me about yourself."

I give him a sharp look. "Do you ever give up?"

"No sugar."

My mouth twitches, and I can't stop it. He notices, and a broad, beautiful smile stretches across his face.

"Girl, you would look real pretty if you smiled."

"Smiling is over rated."

He chuckles softly. "Yeah. How's things going with Jacks?"

I shrug. "Awkward. We hardly know each other."

"He's a good man."

I put stack the glasses and put them into the shelf nearby. "I never said he wasn't."

"He's real proud of you."

I flinch, and then slowly turn back to Cade. "I doubt that."

"He looks at you with pride. We all see it."

I ignore him. There's no point in arguing. If that's what he thinks he can see, then so be it.

"You're safe here, you know that right? Whatever you're running from, it can't touch you here."

I stiffen, but before I can answer him, a sexy female voice fills my ears.

"Cade, there you are."

I peer over my shoulder to see an attractive blonde walking over. She's gorgeous, tatted up and completely rocking the biker chick look. Her tight leather pants fit around her ass like they've been glued on, her top, don't get me started on her top. She might as well take it off; it would probably be less erotic. She saunters over to Cade, grips his shirt and pulls him in for a kiss that has my cheeks flushing. I turn away, not wanting to witness this public display of affection.

"Britney, not now, babe. I'm busy." I hear Cade grunt.

"You said that yesterday, and the day before, there a problem?"

I can't help but listen in, it's hard not to. Is this girl Cade's old lady? It would make sense; she's certainly gorgeous enough to be at his side.

"No, I'm just fuckin' busy."

"Who's the new chick?"

I flinch, knowing full well she's talking about me. I turn, staring over at her. She scowls at me, as she lets her gaze slide over my body. I return the favor, letting her see that there's no way in hell I'm intimidated by her.

"That's Jackson's little girl, best you shut your mouth around her," Cade says.

Britney snorts. "Jackson and me have an understanding. He won't mind me making sure she knows her place around here."

"An understanding?" Cade snorts. "You mean you sucked his dick and earned a moment of respect?"

Yuck.

"Fuck you, Cade. I wouldn't have to suck dick if you just made me your old lady."

Ah, so she's not his old lady. Interesting.

"Not gonna happen, lady, so stop fuckin' tryin'."

"Whatever. I came to tell you Jackson is lookin' for you. It's time for church."

Church, a bikers once a week meeting that they all have to attend, no excuses. Cade stands, ignoring her. He turns, leans over the bar, and flashes me that panty-dropping smile.

"We'll finish our conversation later, sugar."

Then he turns and saunters out looking like God's gift to women. Okay, so the likeliness is that he is, in fact, God's gift. Which just makes it that much harder to look away. I let my eyes swing to Britney, who is now glaring at me. She's giving me the kind of look that suggests it's my fault her piece of ass just walked out. I give her my best smile, turn and walk off, but not before hearing her mumble the one word that tears at my heart strings and has my whole body burning with hurt, even though I don't let it show.

She calls me a whore.

~*~*~*~

"Clean up, then I'll take you home."

I turn and see Jackson leaning against the bar. I've been working here for a week now, and so far things have been good. Most of the guys are kind to me, though they are all very rough. The girls are still unsure, but all of them show a certain level of respect because I'm Jackson's daughter. Fair enough, I suppose, but I would prefer to earn my own respect.

"I'm just going to walk," I say softly, placing the final glass down. Let me tell you, if I have to clean glasses after this experience, I'll stab myself in the eye with a blunt instrument.

37

"You okay, girl?" he asks, straightening and focusing on me.

Jackson has been trying, he really has. He even filled the house with food and put his clothes in the laundry basket instead of all over the house. I know that's an effort for him, and it's an effort I appreciate. We've had a few basic conversations, but mostly, we stay out of each other's way. I feel a certain pull towards Jackson that I'm trying to fight. If I get too close to him, then I'll struggle to walk away, and I know I have to walk away.

"I'm fine, just tired."

He nods, digging into his pocket and pulling out a wad of cash. He hands it to me, and I stare down at it.

"What's this?"

"First weeks' pay."

My hearts swells as I stare down at the cash. To most, this wouldn't be a memorable moment, for me, it's the beginning of my new life. I earned this on my own, without having to rely on another person. This cash, it's all mine.

"Thank you," I breathe, still staring at what has to be at least $500.

"You earned it, now go home, the girls can finish up here."

I nod, and I attempt to give him a smile. He returns it, flashing me what would be an award-winning smile.

"Thanks, Jackson."

He nods, and turns to walk out. When he gets to the door, he glances over at me. "One day, I hope you'll call me Dad." Then he leaves me there, feeling that ache in my heart spread further through my chest. I believe that ache might be the beginnings of something I've never felt for a parent before – I think that ache is love.

Shaking my head and forcing the emotions down, I finish up and pack my things. I'm just heading out the door, when I hear moaning. I don't know if I would call it a natural reaction, or a built in reaction, but I find my curiosity getting the better of me, and I follow the sound. When I step into a large, open room, with a few pool tables and a karaoke machine, I see Cade and Britney. I can't turn my eyes away. I can't because the sight before me is so erotic, my blood heats instantly. My chest begins heaving, and my fingers curl around the doorframe as I peer in, watching them. I shouldn't be watching them, but it's so hard to look away from a sight so utterly...filthy.

Cade is standing against the far wall, his back is to the brick and his fingers are tangled in Britney's hair. She's on her knees, head sliding up and down as she sucks his cock. He doesn't even have his jeans off, they're just open enough to give her access. His eyes are closed, and every now and then he makes a light grunting sound. He looks so delicious standing there like that, eyes closed, head back, chest heaving and skin glistening with a fine layer of sweat. Britney's head bobs faster, and Cade's groans become deeper. I feel my pussy swell and begin a gentle throbbing as all my blood redirects itself.

With a growl, Cade tugs Britney's hair, pulling her back and releasing his cock from her mouth. I let my eyes travel down to the large, hard part of him that's now freed from her mouth. He's massive, not that I expected any less from a man with his build. His cock is covered in a yellow condom, but I can see from the bumps at the ends, that he's pierced. I can't move my eyes away; I don't want to. I just want to stand here and stare at him all day. I watch as he lifts Britney, placing her on a pool table. He lays her down, hoisting her skirt up until she's bare before him. Then he spreads her legs. I swallow a gasp as her pussy comes into sight, glistening, bare and ready for him.

I clench my legs together as the throbbing turns into a painful thud. A huge part of me wants to be the one on that table, feeling his cock sliding in and out of my heat. Cade is the kind of man you want to fuck, just for the experience. Not only is he gorgeous, I also have no doubt he can fuck just as beautifully as he charms women. His body moves like a sleek panther, slow, sexy, prowling. His tongue slides out, wetting his lower lip as he circles the pool table, hand on his cock, stroking gently. I make a light whimpering sound, and that's when he looks up. His eyes meet mine and burn into me. I feel my body jerk, but I don't turn away.

Most women would run, but part of me wants him to know he's been caught. Our eyes hold each other's for a long moment, and I can see that he's still stroking his cock, even though I'm not focusing directly on it. When I finally force my eyes from his, I let them slide down to his hand once more. I take in the sight for a second longer, before taking a step to back out of the room. Cade's eyes widen just a touch, and he grips his jeans, pulling them up over his hard length. Britney notices his movement, and sits up, catching me in the doorway. She smirks, and sits with her legs still parted enough to show her pussy. Seriously?

"Oops, princess caught us."

Why does she assume I'm a princess? Seriously? Do all girls just assume other women they don't know, are bratty? I turn on my heel, deciding now would be a good time to leave them to it. I hear Cade call my name, and then I hear Britney protesting.

"Let her go, Cade. I thought we were going to fuck?"

"Yeah, babe, turns out I'm really not fuckin' interested. Go fuck someone else."

"You were interested a second ago, until she came along!"

He snorts. "No, I was just too fuckin' lazy to pull myself."

"You jerk!"

I grin as I turn the corner and walk to the front door. Cade catches up to me when I am just about at the front gates. I hear his boots crunching in the gravel long before I hear his sexy voice filling my ears.

"You liked what you saw."

It's not a question. It's a simple fact.

"Does it matter if I did, or if I didn't?" I say over my shoulder.

He grips my arm, spinning me around. His green eyes hold mine. God, he's so fucking devastating to look at. He literally makes everything hurt with want.

"It matters, sugar."

"No, it doesn't."

"Does to me, 'coz you know I want inside those panties. I've never wanted inside a girl as much as I want inside you," he drawls.

"Seems like you have plenty of panties to crawl into," I say, grinning at him.

He steps closer, leaning down until I can feel his warm breath against my skin. He smells like beer, and Britney's perfume. It's not off putting though, in fact, it's quite a sexual smell.

"Girls like Britney, they're what you use when doing it yourself is just too hard. They don't feel great, they don't perform great, they're just easy. If I wanted a simple fuck, then sure, I've got plenty of panties to crawl into. I don't want a simple fuck though, I want something that's real. Something like you…"

I cross my arms. "Why the fascination. You don't know me, Cade. Besides, aren't you banned from having sexual relations with the President's daughter?"

"If you had been around the entire time, sure. You haven't, though. Jackson ain't got a say so when it comes to you, so no, there ain't nothin' hold me back from takin' what I want…"

"Why would you want me?" I ask, a little shocked and confused.

"Girls like you are what all men want, sugar."

"You don't know what kind of girl I am, Cade."

"I do," he says, his voice husky. "I know exactly what kinda girl you are."

"Fill me in on that, won't you?"

He leans closer, lifting his heavily ringed fingers to stroke my cheek so lightly, I tremble.

"You're the kind of girl that makes a man want to stop what he's doing, just so he can get a moment to look at that angelic face – a face that will keep him awake for the rest of his fuckin' life. That's the kind of girl you are, sugar."

I swallow, feeling my body coming to life beneath his touch.

"I think you're wrong," I breathe as he leans even closer.

"I'm not wrong. I've seen a lot of people in my life, and I've been with a lot of girls. None of them are as real as you. I'll fuck you, sugar. I'll claim you because you're the meaning of need. You're what I've been lookin' for."

Is he serious? I tremble as he moves even closer, bringing his lips only millimeters from mine. I swallow over and over, trying to think of anything else but him. How could he possibly want me that much, after a mere week and a bit? It's not possible; he doesn't know me. He just wants something different, a challenge perhaps? I don't know, but I do know he's completely wrong about me.

"I'm not what anybody looks for. I'm not what they fight for. I'm not what they breathe for. I'm not the girl you think I am."

He leans down, shocking me as he slides his lips over mine, gently at first, then roughly when I begin to respond. I can't help my hand, as it lifts up to wrap around the chain on his jeans. I tug it, bringing him closer. His boots crunch in the dirt as he takes a step closer, pressing his body against mine. I open my mouth, allowing his tongue to slide in and tangle with mine. His fingers travel up my neck, over my cheek and then he thrusts them into my hair, tangling it around them. The kiss is the kind of kiss that stops your breath, the kind of kiss that stops everything. For a split second, all I can feel is him. When he pulls back, I snake my tongue out and lick the last of him off my bottom lip.

"You might not think you're worth fighting for, or breathing for, but let me tell you, sugar – everyone deserves to be fought for, even those who think they aren't worth it."

Then he lets me go, turns and walks off, leaving me utterly speechless.

Well hell, the biker is deep.

Damn.

~*CHAPTER 4*~

PAST

"Don't fucking bitch at me, Addison."

I stare at my mother, cigarette in her mouth, hair in tangles, wearing nothing but a bra and panties. The man she just serviced is passed out on her bed. He's old and fat. I am guessing he's also rich, by the looks of the suit that's hanging over the back of a nearby chair. Why would any rich man feel the need to put himself anywhere near a woman like my mother? Heck, couldn't he just order a bride or something?

"We have no food, again. You've spent all your money on drugs!"

I am arguing with my mother yet again because there's no food in the house. Once again, she's spent all our money on drugs. She grins at me, showing rotting teeth. "You don't seem to complain about the drugs I buy, considering you make good use of them."

"To avoid reality when your pimp decides he wants a piece of my ass!"

She rolls her eyes. "Don't be so dramatic. Jasper is only giving you what you're allowing him to give."

"Are you fucking serious?" I shout, my voice high and angry.

"Yes, I'm fucking serious," she says in a sing song voice.

Nothing is serious to her, nothing at all. She's just an emotionless soul trapped in a beaten body.

"You know what, I am sick of trying to talk to you. I'll go find my own way to get some food."

"Use that pretty mouth, honey; the men will come running."

I stare at her, completely horrified. "I hope you rot in hell, I really do."

She smirks again. "If I'm goin' to hell, honey, you're comin' with me."

Stupid bitch. I lean down, gripping her purse and opening it. I toss the contents out until I find her stash of money right down the bottom. She thinks I don't know that she keeps bits in there for herself. She lunges at me, screaming loudly as I fist the wad of cash and clench it tightly. Her fingernails slide down my skin as she grips my hair, clawing at me to try and force me to let it go. I slap her hard, and she goes stumbling back. She lunges again, though, ramming my middle section.

"Stupid little whore!" she yells.

"Learned from the best," I growl, attempting to kick her off me once more.

"Whoa, whoa, ladies…"

We both see the fat, ugly man rising from the bed. His belly is hanging far over any parts that may, or may not be, present. I feel the need to throw up. He stands, pulling his pants on with heavy grunts. Then he walks over to the two of us, still squabbling over some cash.

"Jesus, never seen two women fighting like scrawny cats over some cash before. Here," he says, thrusting a fifty at me.

I take the money, letting go of the bundle in my hand. My mother gathers it back up, snarling curses at me. I take a few steps back, clutching the fifty in my hand, not willing to give it back, so the fucker better not change his mind. He stares at me, clutching the money like it's a matter of life or death.

"I'm not takin' it back, girl," he mumbles.

Then I hear him mutter, "Pathetic." And that's exactly how I feel right now, well, most days in fact.

Just pathetic.

"Addison, is it?"

I turn when I hear the sexy, smooth female voice speaking to me. I'm just heading out of the compound after my morning shift at the bar in my second week. I see Britney rushing towards me, blonde hair flapping in the breeze, tits bouncing; the girl really should lock those up. When she stops in front of me, she's panting. She puts a finger up and indicates that I wait while she heaves and catches her breath. Is this bitch serious? I stand there, staring down at her with an amused expression. She straightens once she's caught her breath, and crosses her arms, looking over me. I do the same, giving her my best 'are you finished?' look.

"You're Cade's new flavor, seriously?"

I raise my brows. "I'm sorry, I'm nobody's flavor."

She grins, showing teeth too perfect for her face. They're likely fake. I've been watching her smoke like a chimney all day; it's not possible for them to be that white. "Oh, honey, but you are his flavor. He likes new girls. He likes to play with them, tell them nice things, fuck them, and send them on their way. I'm the only one Cade Duke takes twice."

Cade Duke? What a stupid name.

I give her a rude snort. "That's so nice for you, really. I'm thrilled that you feel so…happy…about being used. I, however, don't get involved with men like Cade and I certainly don't discuss it with his toys."

Her eyes narrow and she scowls. "Be very careful how you speak to me, Addison."

46

"Oh, right, and what are you going to do if I'm not careful?"

She raises her hand, fist bunched, ready to hit me, but I catch the punch mid-air. Her eyes widen, and for a moment, she's stunned. That's all I need, I twist her arm, bringing it around her back, making her bend with a squeal. She cries out loudly.

"Listen to me, lady. If you ever try to lay a hand on me again, I'll break this arm. Unlike you, I have a certain level of respect for myself. If you have a problem with whoring yourself out, that's your business; it ain't mine. I'm here to work, get some money, and leave."

She snarls and curses at me before hissing, "That's not what I heard. I heard your mother was a fucking whore and so are you."

I twist her arm harder and she screams.

"Watch what you say. It's you in the awkward position right now."

"You fucking…"

"Addison!"

Dammit. I glance up to see my father walking towards me, five bikers in tow, one of those bikers is Cade. Jackson rushes over, gripping me and attempting to tug me backwards.

"Let her go," he says to me.

"Bitch was calling me a whore," I yell, twisting Britney's arm harder.

"Just let her go, and I'll deal with it."

"No one calls me a fucking whore!" I hiss.

Hot tears burn under my eyelids and I hate that she's gotten to me. I hate that she tugged my heart strings. Her words aren't true. I know they aren't, but they hurt in a way I can't explain. Jackson gently pries my fingers from Britney's arm. When I let go, she stumbles to the floor with a cry.

"Get up, you're not hurt!" I yell at her, my voice raspy.

"Jackson, I think she broke my arm," she sobs.

Jackson stares down at her, then turns to the bikers behind him. "Jock, Lion, get her back into the house. We'll sort her later."

Two men step forward, hurling Britney up. She wails in pain, but I shoot her a warning look before she's taken away. Jackson spins me around, forcing me to face him. His blue eyes scan my face, a mix of concern and anger.

"Fuckin' hell, girl, you're fuckin' playin' with fire."

I shake his hands from my shoulders, and cross my arms. "She came over and started me, and by the way, I think it's completely rotten that you would go anywhere near that…thing."

He raises his brows. "What I do ain't none of your business. Get home, don't fuckin' start shit like that in my club again."

"And you wonder why I don't call you Dad, a tip for next time, Father – you take your daughter's side," I growl.

Then I spin around and hurry towards the gates, a little hurt but mostly angry. I hear boots crunching behind me, and I turn to see Cade following me. He's grinning at me, completely amused. I growl and turn, continuing on my path without acknowledging him. I don't need his shit right now, nor do I want it. When I'm out onto the road, I can still hear him behind me. Spinning, I bare my teeth in an angry snarl.

"Fuck off, Cade!"

He keeps walking, so I am forced to start walking backwards. His green eyes are dancing with amusement, and he looks extremely

48

powerful as he looms over me. I pick up my pace, walking backwards with greater speed.

"Nice move back there," he says, giving me lusty sex eyes that make me want to place him against the nearest tree and take his cock into my mouth and suck until he comes hard in my mouth…fuck…I shouldn't be thinking like that. Get him out of your head, Addison.

"She had it coming."

He nods, as if agreeing. "I have no doubt. She has a big mouth."

"I bet."

He gives a deep, throaty laugh. "Sassy little thing, aren't ya, sugar?"

"Stop calling me sugar. Do I look sweet to you?"

He reaches out, gripping my shoulders and stopping me. He leans in close and murmurs, "You might not look sweet, but I bet you taste fuckin' sweet."

"Seriously?" I whisper. "You're hitting on me in the middle of a road?"

"I like to do it in style," he says, staring at my lips.

"Are you always this full on when you want to get your dick wet?"

He grins, slow and sexy. "Sugar, if I wanted my dick wet, I could get it wet anywhere, with anyone. I don't want my dick wet. I want it fuckin' drenched, drippin' and surrounded in you."

I swallow, feeling my cheeks flush. "You'll have to do a little better than dirty lines on a road if you want anywhere near me."

He reaches out, running his thumb across my lower lip. "But you already want me. I can see it. I can smell it."

Smell it? Is he serious?

"I think what you can smell," I say, taking a step back, "is the last whore you drenched yourself in."

He lashes out, gripping my shoulder again and stopping me from moving back. "Keep speakin', baby, it only makes me want you more."

I peel his fingers from my shoulders. "If you don't mind, I really have some things to do."

"Like?"

I scowl at him. "That's none of your business."

"I'm makin' it my business, what you doin'?"

I raise my brows. "I'm going into town, alone."

"No, you're not. I'm takin' you."

"Um, no you're not."

"Um, yeah, sugar. I am."

I cross my arms and he does the same, staring down at me with a determined expression.

"No. You're. Not."

He leans closer.

"Yes. I. Am."

"Seriously!" I cry, throwing my hands up. "You're impossible."

He grins, pleased with himself. "I know, now, let me go and get my bike. I'll be back in ten."

"Oh, hell no! I'm not getting on a death trap."

He chuckles. "How were you plannin' on gettin' in there?"

I roll my eyes. "Walking, duh!"

He bursts out laughing. "Did you not pay attention when you were comin' in? Closest town is at least thirty miles."

Dammit.

"Well, I'll borrow Jackson's car."

"Jackson don't have a car, sugar."

Fuck.

I throw my hands up, and in an exasperated tone, I snap, "Fine, you win!"

He grins, spinning around and sauntering back towards the compound. "See you in ten, sugar."

Fucking asshole.

~*CHAPTER 5*~

PRESENT

When Cade shows up on his Harley, I stare at it for a long, long moment. He's not serious? He wants me to get on that? I won't lie and say it's not sexy as hell, with its chrome fittings and candy-apple red paint but really? It looks so...dangerous. Cade gets off. The buckles on his boots make a clinking sound as he walks towards me. His eyes scan over my outfit. I had to find the closest thing to riding clothes that I could. I got jeans, and a tank, and a pair of old runners. It's the best I could piece together. I don't have many clothes to choose from.

"That all you got to wear?" he says, in an almost disgusted tone.

I cross my arms, feeling suddenly ugly. "Yes, it is."

"No leathers?"

"Serious?" I snort.

"Fuckin' deadly serious, sugar," he says, his eyes hard.

"Then no, I don't."

"Fine, we're gettin' some."

"I can't afford leathers," I protest as he thrusts a helmet at me and gets back on the bike.

"I can, now get on."

I slide on the back of the bike, feeling my heart leap into my throat.

"You're not buying me anything; this is the one and only time I'm getting on this bike."

He grips my knees, pulling me forward so my legs are spread and his back is rested comfortably between them. He runs a hand up my thigh until he reaches my ass, he grips it, pressing me even closer to him. I swallow, smothering a whimper as the leather on his jacket rubs suggestively against my pussy. Fuck. He grips my wrists next, pulling them around his large, solid body. When I connect them at the front, I realize how close my face is to his back. I can smell him, and fuck, he smells like man dipped in chocolate, covered with fuckable sprinkles.

"Hold on, sugar."

He starts the bike, and the rumble goes right to my core. I close my eyes, clenching my teeth as the vibrations do wonderful things to my already soaked pussy. I shift on the seat, uncomfortable with how aroused this man is making me. I'm an extremely sexual person; it's hard not to be when you've lived a life based around sex. I haven't had a great deal of good sex in my time, most of it was drunken sex, high sex, or forced sex. I don't remember a great deal of the forced sex with Jasper, probably because I used to get so high it would knock me out. The only good sex I ever had, was with Billy, my ex-boyfriend. My first love, my first heart break, my first decent sexual experience.

Cade turns his head looking me dead in the eye. "Your little pussy against my back is doin' bad things to me, sugar. Keep still."

I squirm at his words, and his eyes flare.

"Keep fuckin' still," he grates out. "Or I'll have them jeans around your ankles in less than five minutes and my dick will be buried deep inside that hot little cunt."

I open my mouth, shocked and completely aroused. Cade turns, lifting his boots and pulling the throttle. The bike lurches forward; my thoughts quickly disappear and a scream escapes my throat. I feel Cade's chuckle rumble through his back and into my chest. I hold on tighter, terrified and completely thrilled, all in one. I scream, squeal and then laugh as he picks up speed, heading towards town. My hair whips around, the wind tickles my face, and for a moment, I feel completely free. It's a moment in my life, I know I'll never forget. The freedom I feel on this bike, is a freedom I've never felt. It's exhilarating. It's one of the most beautiful, intense feelings I've ever had pulsing through my chest. As we soar along, the rumble of the Harley the only sound we hear, I ponder how I will keep Cade at a distance. He doesn't seem like the kind of man to give up easily if he wants something.

It's clear Cade isn't about to give up on me; obviously, he's found a fascination. I won't lie and say he's not doing crazy things to my body, but I'm not here to get involved. I am here to try and make another life for myself and move on from my past. I can't get tangled up. I have to stay focused on my plan. I don't need any more drama or things keeping me held back. I stare at the trees whizzing past me, and I know how easily I could get comfortable here, with Jackson and this life, but I can't do that. Living this kind of lifestyle isn't putting me forward, it's just keeping me at a standstill, and I can't allow that.

I feel Cade's bike slowing, and I peer at the town ahead. It's only small, maybe five or six thousand people by the looks of it. I suppose it's what you would call an outback town; it's got that outback kind of look about it and by the way people are dressed, definitely that kind of feel too. Cade pulls up his bike, and I slip off the back. My legs wobble and I reach out, gripping the seat to steady myself. Cade chuckles and slips his helmet off, and then grips mine and pulls it off my head. I stare up at him, and when he's smiling down at me the way he is now, it makes it that much harder to just turn everything off.

"Your legs will do that for a bit after gettin' off a bike."

I nod, standing straight. "Can you tell me where there are some decent shops in this place?"

He raises a brow. "You're not serious?"

Now I raise my brow. "Of course, what did you think I came here for?"

"Fucks me, a drink? Something to eat?"

"I need decent shoes for a start, and something to wear to work. My feet kill me all day in that bar."

Cade is still staring at me, looking completely shocked. Did the man honestly think I wanted to come in here, to get a drink? Shocker. I can't help the smile that creeps across my face as he runs his hand through his hair, ruffling it with his fingers. He's completely and utterly distressed about this, and it's completely and utterly thrilling to me that I've gotten him all wound up. Score one, Addison.

"You want me to go girly shopping with you?" he says, in a rather horrified voice.

I giggle, and it sounds so completely off for me. I skip past Cade with a grin as big as Mount Everest. "You offered, hot stuff."

With a grunt, he reluctantly follows me. For the first time in days, I can't wipe the smile off my face. The big tough biker is going shopping with me!

~*CHAPTER 6*~

PAST

I feel a set of hands tugging my pants, and I jerk upright. My forehead slams into someone else's and I yelp. It takes me a moment to realize where I am and what's happening. When I do, I realize that some filthy client is trying to crawl into my bed and score some off me. I blink rapidly, gripping my pants and trying to gain some control. It's hard when you're only sixteen, and you try to fight off a man twice your size and age. The stranger grunts, and grips my hands, trying to force them above my hand as he positions himself over me.

"Get off me!" I cry.

"Paid for service, going to fuckin' get it," he slurs.

He's drunk. That's not uncommon; a lot of clients are drunk. A lot of clients are twisted and fucked up. Let's face it, if you're normal, you don't need to pay the scum of the earth for sex.

"Get off me," I repeat, shoving and squirming.

"Be five minutes, I paid good money."

"Then I'll give you your money back," I protest, trying to raise my knees up as he shifts his body, pressing himself between my legs.

"Stupid whore in there already spent it, so I guess you better give me what I need."

"Fuck off!" I cry, biting down onto the closest piece of flesh I can get my mouth around. I think it's his shoulder. It makes me want to gag.

He roars, and then he slaps me so hard my head spins. As he moves though, I bring my knee up and kick him hard in the groin. When he stumbles off the bed with a hiss, I leap up, flicking the lamp on. I've learned how to deal with clients like this, who decide I'm the next best thing if they aren't serviced by my mother. The first one I ever had, came at me when I was fourteen, I didn't have the experience then, and he raped me. I learned quickly after that. There's only one man that gets away with it now, and that's Jasper. The only reason he gets away with it, is because he's our lifeline. Without him, we're on the streets. Pathetic, I know.

I get off the bed just as the man is rising off the floor. It shocks me to see he's quite well groomed. He's wearing suit pants. Okay, they're not expensive looking, by any stretch, but it's still a suit. He's got salt and pepper hair, and is quite well built. Before he can lash out at me, I drive my foot into his nose. The sickening crunch, followed by blood spurting is a familiar sound and sight for me. He roars in pain as blood flows down his face.

"Little fuckin' bitch," he bellows.

"Get the fuck out of my house. You're not the first pervert to try and get into my bed, and you won't be the last. I will cut your dick off if you try and touch me ever again."

He crawls towards the door, and blood drips in a trail on the old faded carpet as he goes. When he gets to the door, he turns and looks at me. He's panting, in both pain and anger. He covers his nose with one hand, and uses the other to support himself.

"Whore," he growls.

Then he crawls out the door. The word has my body trembling. It's the one word I can't deal with, no matter how many times I hear it.

It's the one thing I never want to be.

And yet, sometimes, I wonder if it's inevitable.

~*PRESENT*~

"Jesus woman, remind me never to offer you a ride into town again," Cade grumbles as we head out of the last store later in the day.

I'm happy. I have two new pairs of shoes and a couple of work outfits. Cade bought me a leather jacket, and it was the only moment that he smiled. The rest of the time he grumbled and muttered under his breath. This only made me smile more, and take a heck of a lot longer to find what I needed. I turned a one hour trip into a two hour trip, and I enjoyed every second of it.

"Well, next time you won't be so pushy when a woman says she's going into town," I say, satisfied with myself.

"Damn right," he mutters.

I smile again, and when we reach his bike, he tosses me a helmet and secures the bags in the two panniers on either side of the bike. I slip the helmet on, and when he gets on the bike, I slide on behind him. I wrap my arms around his waist and take a moment to breathe him in. I'm completely flattered that Cade spent the whole afternoon with me, even though he didn't have to. He may have grumbled like a bitch in heat, but he did it, and that warms parts deep inside me. Cade grips my fingers, taking a moment to slide his roughened fingertips over mine. I shiver, feeling my body come alive. I want Cade, no amount of denying that will do me any good.

"Fuck," I hear him mutter, before starting up the bike.

I smile into his back knowing how easily I affect him. I also know how much he affects me. When he speeds off onto the street, I tremble with excitement and pure happiness. I'll never get over the way this bike makes me feel, the way my heart thuds, the way my body becomes relaxed and full of joy, the way I feel so completely at ease. When we hit the highway, I swallow down the anxious feeling that creeps into my chest. I want Cade, and after today, I want him to know it. I know I really shouldn't be getting involved with anyone, but from what I see of Cade, he's only up for a bit of fun. I could use a bit of fun right now. I haven't been with another man since…well…Billy. He was one of the only men I let come near me, that I actually enjoyed being around.

I feel Cade's stiff body, and I know he's feeling the same sexual tension I am. I reach further around him, wondering if what I'm about to do is going to shock him into a crash? Surely not. I slide my fingers down his hard, firm chest until I reach the top of his jeans. I grip them, gently undoing the button. He stiffens even more, but he doesn't move to stop me. I unzip him, and then I slip my hand inside. He jerks when I find his erect cock and wrap my fingers around it. Cade is thick, long and pierced. He has the kind of cock that makes women beg for more, slightly titled up, thick head, and those silver barbells in the perfect locations. I squeeze him and feel him pulse beneath my palm.

I clench my legs around his thighs as my pussy aches, begging for attention. I begin a gentle stroking and I hear Cade's grunt. He lets one hand off the handle bars, and he grips my hand, stopping me. He jerks my fingers from his cock and pulls my hands out of his jeans. I feel my heart plummet to my belly. He doesn't want me? Had I been reading this all wrong? God, I'm such a fool. Cade stays on the highway a moment longer, then suddenly he's turning off. I see a long, gravel road and at the end, is a large, white home. He speeds down the road, and skids to a stop outside the house. He turns the bike off, and gets off quickly and angrily. I let him go, not moving, not daring to remove my helmet. He tears his helmet from his head and hurls it across the dirt, then he grips mine, repeating the process.

Holy shit. Cade is gorgeous when he's aroused and angry. Part of me doesn't quite understand his anger, perhaps it's because he know this isn't really the right thing for us to be doing, and he's been trying to fight it? He stalks towards me, his body wound up, his eyes flaring with lust. He reaches me, grips my hips and lifts, spinning me around so my back is against the handle bars. He steps over the bike, facing me, takes my shoulders and pulls me close. His eyes hold mine, so intense, so green, so full of sex and desire. He runs his thumb over my bottom lip, and then he brings his mouth down over mine. Electric bolts shoot through me as his mouth moves angrily against mine. When his tongue slides out, I accept it, full and deep. One of his hands grips my hip, and the other he uses to cup my pussy through my jeans.

I groan into his mouth when he tilts his hand, rubbing in that perfect way. My body begs for attention as he tears his mouth from mine and slides his lips down my neck. I forget everything in this moment. I forget that we're on a bike, in front of some house I don't know. I forget that I shouldn't be doing this. I forget about my past, and my mother. I just exist in this moment with Cade, and I want it more than I want to breathe. I tangle my fingers into his hair, jerking his head back so I can capture his mouth again. He tastes divine, his tongue so soft, his lips so full. That little lip ring tickles my lips in the most impeccable way. He grips my jeans and unbuttons them; I jerk and tear my lips from his.

"Here?" I rasp.

"Here. Now. I need to fuck you. I need my cock deep inside you. So fuckin' gorgeous, so fuckin' edible."

He makes short work of my shoes first, then he pulls at my jeans, and drags them down my legs. I shift my backside, lifting my legs, so he can remove them completely. Cade makes a strangled sound and returns my legs so they're back either side of his bike. He pushes my chest gently, and I rest my back against the handle bars. He grips each of my ankles, lifting them to rest on the pegs, then he grips my knees and spreads them wide. I whimper when his eyes set on my exposed pussy. The hiss that escapes his lips tells me that he likes what he's seeing. He stretches his hand out, sliding a finger through the arousal coating my slick sex, and then he slips it into his mouth. I make a whining sound watching him lick my arousal off his finger.

"Fuckin' beautiful, sugar," he rasps.

"God, more," I beg.

"Goin' to fuckin' eat that gorgeous little cunt, you ready, baby?"

"Yes, fuck, yes."

He grips my hips, titling them up and then he leans down. As his tongue slides through my heat, I cry out, thrusting up to meet the next delectable lick. He growls against my skin, and then clamps his teeth over my swollen clit, gently rolling it between them while his tongue flickers the end. I've never had something so fucking amazing in my life. I scream out as pleasure builds at a rapid pace. Holy shit, I've never needed to come so hard in my life. I feel his finger slide inside me, and tilt at that perfect angle. I lose it. The first burst of my orgasm is intense. I lose all ability to contain my screams. I thrash my head from side to side, crying out his name. He licks and sucks every last shudder from my body, before lifting his head and letting his tongue slide out across his lips, licking my arousal off.

"So fuckin' wet, nicest tastin' pussy I've ever put my mouth on."

I quiver. My eyes are hooded as I watch him jerk his jeans down just enough to release his cock. He reaches into his back pocket for a condom, and then he tears it open with his mouth before rolling it onto his hard length. Now sheathed, he steps closer, takes my ankles and puts them around his hips. He presses close to me, his head just probing my center.

"Want this sugar?" he growls.

"Yes, please, stop teasing me."

"Tell me what you want, word for word. Make me want it, baby."

"I want your cock," I whimper. "I want your beautiful cock inside me, hard, fast, and deep."

He groans, "Fuck, you're sexy."

He slides the tip of his cock into my pussy and I arch, oh God, yes. He slides in another inch; I groan his name and hold the grips on the handlebars so tightly my fingers ache. Fully stretched around him, I forget everything else but this moment. He slides his hips back, the entire length of him leaving me, then he thrusts back in. I moan and reach up under my shirt to tweak my nipples.

"Fuck, get those babies out for me, sugar," Cade orders, his voice hoarse.

I grip my shirt, and pull it up to reveal my small, but perky breasts. He hisses, and his thrusts become quicker. He leans over, sucking one of my hard nipples into his mouth while his other hand slips underneath me. For a moment, I don't know what he's doing until the bike roars to life. The vibrations that rip through my body does crazy things to me. I scream and jerk, as the combination of his thrusting and the vibrations coming off the bike, send me over the edge. I clamp around him, coming with such force I don't recognize my own cries. All I can feel is the deep, blinding, pulsating jerks of pleasure taking over my body.

"Mother fucker," Cade grunts. "So fuckin' tight."

I know the moment he comes; I can feel his cock pulsing, I'm wrapped that tightly around him. He doesn't make a sound. He just buries his head into my chest and thrusts until he's got nothing left. Then, he just lays there for the longest moment, catching his breath. I do the same, running my fingertips through his thick, dark hair as I come down from what is easily the best sex I've ever had.

"Fuck, girl, you were so fuckin' tight, that was so fuckin' mind blowing. I never thought...just...wow."

Okay! That's a random thing to say. You were so tight? Who says that?

"What did you expect," I joke lightly. "A big, loose fuck?"

He doesn't say anything, and I realize what he meant. It hits me so hard, I jerk violently under him. Cade thinks the rumors are true. He thinks I was a whore. Feeling my vision blur, I struggle to push him off me. He seems confused as he pulls back, but when he sees my face, it doesn't take him long to click.

"I didn't..."

I pull my hand back, and I punch him so hard I hear his jaw crack. He roars in pain, and stumbles backwards, only just managing to steady the bike. I scramble off, gripping my jeans and pulling them back on. Cade is still snarling as he kicks the stand on his bike and storms towards me. I throw my hands up, and they tremble as I try to hold them out in front of me.

"Come near me again, you mother fucker, and I'll put you on your ass. Don't think I can't," I snarl.

"What the fuck?" he snaps, rubbing his jaw.

"How dare you!" I scream. "You thought I was a fucking whore! You fucked me because you thought I was easy?"

He stares at me, his green eyes intense as he scans my face. "I didn't fuckin' say that..."

"My mother was a fucking whore, so you assumed I was the same. You heard I have been fucking since I was thirteen so you assumed that I had been paid for it. You fucking asshole, you piece of shit! I actually liked you!"

I spin and begin storming down the drive. Cade runs after me.

"Addison, stop!"

"Fuck you, Cade. How could you? I know you're a biker. I know you get around, but how could you treat me like that?"

My voice is hoarse and I hate it. I hate he's dragged this kind of emotion from me. My entire body is shaking. My palms are sweating and everything inside me aches. I'm hurt. It's been a long time since I've felt such intense hurt. How could I let him affect me like this? After a few short days, I let myself become attracted to him; I let myself think he was different. He isn't. None of them are. I should know that by now.

"Addison, I didn't...fuck...just listen."

I spin around. "Do you want to know how many men I've fucked, Cade?"

"No, fuck, I just..."

"I've fucked three, and been raped by one."

His eyes widen, and I continue before he can speak.

"You're one of those three, Cade. The other was a regular fuck and he was good to me, the last was my boyfriend Billy. The man who raped me, also took my virginity at thirteen, and continued to assault me until Billy came along and stopped him. I'm a sexual person, I won't lie about that. I like to fuck. I like to explore, but I don't do it with just anyone. I've only trusted two people enough, and both times I enjoyed it, but it was nothing like what I felt just then. You came along, and you seemed to want me, you seemed genuine, and I felt the attraction, so I thought why not? Why not pick someone who I actually feel a deep sexual attraction to? I wanted to see what it was like, to feel you around me and maybe, just maybe, feel like I wasn't being used, but really it was just a cheap, quick fuck," I spit the words at him, they fly from my mouth like venom.

He stares at me, completely shocked. "Fuck, sugar, I wasn't..."

"Take me home, Cade," I demand, clenching my fists.

His eyes scan my face, and for a moment, he looks like he's going to back down, but he doesn't. Instead, his face hardens and he walks over, stopping in front of me.

"No," he says simply.

"Don't fuck with me, Cade. I want to go."

"I said, no," he says, his voice firm.

"You don't get a say so in this, you insult me and then…"

"Shut up."

I feel my eyes widen. "Excuse me?"

He steps forward, leaning in so close I can almost taste him. "I said, shut up."

"How fucking dare you-"

He covers my mouth with his hand. I squirm and attempt to open my mouth enough to get my teeth around his skin. My attempts fail, and I squirm and grunt behind Cade's hand.

"Listen to me, and listen good," he says, a flicker of compassion crosses his features before he replaces it with anger. "Don't pretend to know what I'm thinkin'. I didn't say one fuckin' word about you bein' a whore. You asked a question that question shocked me. I don't have to explain myself to you, because I didn't think what you assumed I was thinkin'. I don't judge, no matter what shit goes down in someone's life. We all got a past, girl, and we all have skeletons. Ain't my place to judge another's history. I wanted and enjoyed every fuckin' second of having my cock buried inside you, so it's about time you shut up, and stop blowin' off the handle at people before they get a chance to explain. We ain't here to be your enemies, sugar. We're here to protect you. It's about time you learned some trust."

65

He lets my mouth go. I take a few steps back and pant with rage and hurt.

"I don't trust," I say angrily.

He steps closer, burning me with his gaze, his fists are clenched. I can just about hear him panting. "You do now, 'coz I am the kinda man who don't fuck someone over. I can hate a fucker, but I don't fuck him over. I got somethin' to say, I say it. I don't dance around. I don't lie and I don't play games."

I open my mouth to speak, but he puts a hand up and stops me. His expression is thunderous and wild.

"And one other thing," he growls, "ever fuckin' lay a hand on me again, I'll drop you on your ass. I don't hit women, fuck, I'd kill any fucker that did, but my theory is, if you got the nuts to fuckin' hit a man, you are askin' for trouble. Don't do it again. Now get on the fuckin' bike."

I stare at him, shocked. His words hit me at my very core. They cut me deep because they're so incredibly real. I can brush off abuse, I can brush off fake, but real words that hit my soul, they hurt. Fuck, they burn. My legs wobble as I walk towards the bike, completely unable to focus on the road in front of me. My eyes burn like fire, the tears threaten to escape over my eyelids and slip down my cheeks, showing my weakness. Cade gets onto the bike, starts it up and pulls the throttle, flicking rocks across the lawn. He turns his face to me, his eyes are wild and I can see he's beyond angry.

"Get on the bike, now," he growls.

I pull the helmet over my head, and with trembling legs, I get on the bike. As soon as my feet are off the ground, Cade takes off. Rocks fling about, hitting us as he tears down the road. When he skids out onto the highway, I have to grip his jacket to stop myself from falling. I can feel him panting beneath my fingertips, he's angry and I know I deserve his anger. I assumed he thought something he didn't, but right now he's scaring me. I close my eyes, take a deep breath and focus on the wind whipping my face and the sound of the bike roaring as Cade picks up speed. We'll be there soon; it'll all be fine.

Finally, we pull into the compound. I skitter off the bike so quickly I end up on my ass in the dirt. I get to my feet swiftly, shove my helmet at Cade, turn and storm out of the gates toward my father's house. I don't look back, and Cade doesn't follow. It's for the best; we both know it too. I don't need anything holding me back, and Cade clearly doesn't want it. We made a mistake, having sex on the back of his bike earlier. We took that step from flirting to taking action, and taking action fucks things up. It confuses things. It makes things difficult and awkward. I should have ignored my lust, did what I had to do, and moved on.

But I didn't, and that's on me.

~*CHAPTER 7*~

PAST

I can smell his sweat as he moves over me; his body plunges inside of mine. Bile rises and falls over and over in my throat. I've learned to hold it down. There's no point in letting it out; it'll only make him angrier and the prick gets horny when he's angry. I just hold my breath and let the drugs in my system take me to another world. It's the only way to survive this. The only way to survive the suffocating feeling of having him all over me, having his body thrusting into mine, hearing his grunts. God, I wish it would end. I just want it to be over. Things would be so much easier if I were dead.

"What the fuck!"

I hear the sound, and I feel the mass of relief flood through my body. Billy. He came for me like he promised he would. Before I have the chance to open my eyes, Jasper is launched into a nearby wall. Billy has hold of his now limp cock and he twists it. The sound Jasper makes is that of pure agony, and yet it brings me complete comfort. Watching Jasper being lowered to his knees, is a sight I will never forget and will be forever grateful for. Billy leans down and drives his fist into Jasper's nose over and over until thick red blood spurts out and coats the walls. I don't even flinch. I have no feelings towards this, none at all.

"You ever fucking touch her again, I will come to you in the night and slice your cock off and fuck you with it until you're bleeding, you rotten piece of shit. Do you understand me?"

Jasper grunts. His face is red and he's sweating. "Fuck you!"

Billy twists Jasper's cock so hard, the roar that comes from his mouth is ear splitting.

"Okay," Jasper rasps, his voice broken. "I won't touch her."

"If it wasn't for her Momma, you would be dead right now, you piece of shit. If you take this out on them though, mark my words, I'll gut you."

Jasper nods, his face bloated, red and now dripping. He's panting, his mouth is twisted in a way that's gone beyond pain. Billy lets him go, puts his foot to Jasper's chest and sends him backwards into the wall. Jasper scrambles to his knees, and scurries out the door. When he's gone, Billy turns to me. He's literally shaking with rage and his brown eyes are flaring open and closed with emotion.

"How long?" he says in a voice so icy, I flinch.

"Since I was thirteen."

"You never told me?" he roars and paces the room, fists clenched with rage.

"I didn't want to risk my mother."

"Your mother?" he bellows, spinning around. "That woman put you in this mess."

I stand, pulling a sheet around myself. "And she is all I have. Without her, I won't survive."

"You'll survive with me!"

"And what if that goes wrong?"

His eyes narrow and he runs a hand through his sandy-blonde hair. "Is that all you think of this? Of us?"

"I've seen what happens to love. I've seen married men come in and have their dicks sucked because their wives are tired or looking after children. I've seen women coming in looking for company, because their husbands work too much. I know where love goes, and I won't risk it. So yes, that is what I think of this."

He shakes his head sadly. "Addison, you're letting this ruin you. One day, a man is going to come along and sweep you away. He's going to give you that feeling you can't go back on, that feeling that will change your world. You won't think like this then."

"It won't happen," I say, feeling my eyelids become heavy as I begin to come down from my high.

"Not even with me?"

I stare at him through hooded lashes. "You're as close as I've ever come to love, Billy. It's not enough though. I am what I am. You're better off moving on and finding something worth fighting for."

"You're worth fighting for, Addison."

"In your eyes, perhaps."

He looks pained now. "Why don't you stop him?"

I shrug, light up a cigarette and sit down. "What's the point? He's going to do it, even if I fight. He knows he'll get what he wants, because without him, my mother and I are on the streets. He needs her, and with her comes me. He knows I won't fight. It's just quicker if I block it out."

"He's raping you," he whispers, disgusted.

"Yeah, well, there are worse things in the world."

"Addison, will there ever come a time you'll let someone save you?"

I stand, walk past him and head toward my bedroom. At the door, I turn back to him. "Saving someone only works if that person wants or deserves to be saved."

"Have you looked at yourself lately?" he yells. "Have you?"

"Yes!"

"No, you haven't! Addison, you're sinking. You need to take a good hard look at yourself, this isn't how you want to be, God dammit, wake up."

Before I know what he's doing, he's got me and drags me into the bathroom. He flicks on the light and shoves me in front of the broken glass. "Look!"

I stare at the girl in the mirror, the girl with hollow cheeks, dark rings under her eyes, and ratty hair that holds no color. She's broken; she's damaged. When did I let myself become so...so horrible? I swallow down the bile that rises in my throat. Who is that girl in front of me?

She's not me.

I know what she is.

She's a nothing.

~*PRESENT*~

"Have you seen Cade?" I ask Jackson one afternoon, about two weeks into my stay.

Cade hasn't spoken a lot to me since I over reacted at him, and while I understand it, it's kind of pissing me off.

Jackson nods, and points towards a small shed up the back of the lot.

"He's workin' on his bike."

"Thanks."

"What you need him for?" he asks, wiping some grease onto his jeans.

I avoid his gaze. "Just to chat."

71

"No woman just chats with Cade. Be careful, Addison. He's not the kind of man that will change your life."

I stare up at him, and then I narrow my eyes. "Someone probably said that about you once, Jackson. It doesn't mean it's true."

"Look where love got me."

I turn and walk towards the small shed. "Who said love had anything to do with this?"

Jackson doesn't get to answer, and that's fine by me. I don't want to hear his answer. Not right now. I know it'll only be something that makes my heart hurt. I reach the small shed, and can hear the sounds of tools tinkering. I grip the handle, open the door and step inside. It's only a small space, and in the middle, Cade's bike is hoisted up and he's standing underneath it, completely shirtless. I stop walking, and I let my eyes travel over his body. Hot damn, what a body it is. Cade is ripped in a way a girl can only dream about. Broad shoulders, tight chest, washboard abs and that sexy-as-sin man 'V'. He's covered from head to toe in streaks of grease.

"Jackson told me I would find you here," I say, and he stops what he's doing to turn and stare at me.

"If I wanted to be found," he says, turning his spanner, "I wouldn't be down here with the door closed."

Well excuse me. I walk over and stop next to his bike. I run my fingers over the shiny paint. Cade stares at me, his head slightly tilted to the side. He drops his tools, and wipes his hands on his jeans before stepping in front of me.

"What do you want, sugar?"

Well, at least he's calling me sugar, that's a start.

"To apologize."

He raises his brows. "Didn't think you were the type to apologize."

72

This just makes me angry. I've come in here to admit I'm wrong, yet he's mocking me and playing games.

"You know what, if you're going to be a jerk-off, I won't apologize. Go fuck yourself, Cade."

I turn, but he grips my arm and spins me back around. He presses my body to his, and I can feel his hot skin against what little of mine is exposed.

"You always run off when things don't go your way?" he murmurs.

"I'm not a typical female, biker. I'm not going to get on my knees and beg for your forgiveness. I'm not going to follow you around hoping you will talk to me again. If you're pissed at me, then I'm not going to fight to change it."

"So fuckin' stubborn," he says, and wraps an arm around my lower back. He presses me even closer.

"Do you mind? Let me go."

"I don't mind at all, and no."

"Cade..."

"Sugar..."

"You're so fucking frustrating," I protest, squirming.

"And you're so fuckin' gorgeous, tryin' to fight me all the time."

I stare up at him, and he looks down at me with a heated expression. I can see his lust, heck, I can feel his lust. It's pressing against my belly, hard and pulsing.

"Let me go," I say, though my voice has lost its spark.

"You don't really want that, sugar."

73

"Yes, I do. Don't flatter yourself into thinking I want you, Cade. You're attractive. I liked being with you, but that's where it ends. I was only coming to apologize for being a bitch the other day, end of story."

"Such a fuckin' liar," he says, in a husky tone.

He's staring at my lips now. Dammit. Why does he have to look at me like that? It weakens my resolve.

"You're living a delusional life, biker."

He gives me a lazy half smile. "And you're thinkin' about my cock all deep and hard inside you."

I attempt to roll my eyes, but I have no doubt I look extremely spastic. This would be because my breath hitches at the same time my eyes move. The reason? Cade's hand is now covering my pussy. The sneaky bastard managed to slip it around when I was arguing. He's cupping me, pressing just enough to give me tingles of pleasure.

"You know I'm right," he growls. "I can feel how fuckin' wet you are."

"Delusional," I rasp.

"You'd like it if I bent you over right now, slipped those jeans down and slid my cock into that delectable little cunt."

I swallow and my cheeks heat. I want to answer, but my body is pulsing and all I can feel is his hand rocking over my pussy.

"Yo' Cade!"

Before I know what's happening, Cade steps back, and I sway on my feet. The door swings open and two bikers step in. I'm still learning all their names, but from what I can remember, it's Yank and Quinn. I don't know why they call the tall man Yank, but most of the bikers have a nickname. Though I haven't heard them call Cade by one.

"What the fuck do you want?" Cade grumbles.

"Jackson needs to talk with you."

Of course he does. I sigh and turn. "I'll see you later."

"Wait up, sugar," Cade says, but I don't stop – let him think I don't care.

I smile the entire way back to the compound, though he will never know that.

~~*~*~

"Give us another round, girl."

I turn, hands full, and see another biker wanting beer. The girl I'm working with tonight, Mindy, is late. Again. The bitch never shows up on time. The only reason she still has a job, is because Jackson can't convince any normal woman to work with a bunch of rude, feral bikers. I juggle the drinks already in my hand as I place them down on the counter and slide them towards the waiting biker. He flashes me a quick grin, then turns away. I begin to gather the next order, feeling sweat trickle down my face as I become flustered with the amount of work I'm trying to squeeze in.

"Okay, where are we at?"

I turn to see Mindy walking in, tits bulging out of her white top, shorts so tiny her ass cheeks hang out. I sigh, roll my eyes and then snap, "Did you ever think of coming to work on time?"

She puts her hands up, flicks her blonde hair over her shoulder and widens her blue eyes. "Hey, I was busy."

"What was it this time, Mindy? Your dog died? Your cat ate your budgie? Oh wait, what was it yesterday? Oh, that's right, all the tires on your car blew off."

75

She crosses her arms. "They actually did all burst, someone punctured them."

"Well, maybe you should show up to work instead of causing trouble and people wouldn't feel the need to puncture your tires."

She glares at me, turns and begins taking orders. Well, at least I can finally take my break. I throw the towel off my shoulder down onto the counter, and turn, yelling out as I walk off. I'm just about to turn down the hall, when a hand reaches out and grips me. I'm pulled into a hard, firm body and I break out in shivers all over as Cade presses me against a nearby wall. I've been making it my mission to avoid him since the afternoon in the shed. I know it's annoying him, but I don't want him to see that he affects me how he does. There's going to come a point where I can no longer say no to him.

"What the hell, Cade? You can't just pull me into a dark hall and do what you want!" I snarl.

"Sugar," he growls. "You're fuckin' with me. You know I'm watching. You know it and you're still doin' it. Watching me from the corner of your eye, givin' me those sexy little stares. I can see it, and fuck, you know I want it."

"I am not…"

"Seein' you out there, smilin' at the men as you serve beers makes me fuckin' angry. I want to take you, then and there, and slam you against the wall and let everyone here know you're mine. I want to spread your legs and drive my cock deep, claiming you, owning you."

"Cade, you're insa…"

"Sugar, shut the fuck up. You know you're my girl now. You've known that since the day I took you on the back of my bike. I don't just take girls like that. If I wanna fuck, that's just what I do, but it

76

ain't never like that. You're callin' for me, and I can't look back. I need to claim you, and now you're playin' with me."

"You might have claimed me," I growl. "But I didn't claim you."

"Did you take my cock?"

"What? You know the answer to that," I snap, frustrated.

"Then you claimed me, too."

"Cade, you're fucking delusion-"

"I warned you once," he growls, cutting me off. "I won't fuckin' do it again. Shut the fuck up, sugar. Now, I'm gonna kiss you 'coz I've been without those sweet lips while you play stupid little bullshit games with me. I won't be without for another minute. Open your lips, baby, and kiss me."

He doesn't let me answer; he simply grips the back of my head, tangles his fingers into my hair, and pulls me close. I expect his lips to crash down over mine, but he just grazes them across, causing shivers to run down my spine. Cade knows I want him, he's known since the day I laid on his bike and let him claim me. He sees something deep inside me, a want that I don't recognize fully yet, and he's pulling it from me, both hands wrapped tightly around it. I lean into him, wanting to deepen the kiss, but he pulls back. He tastes so good, just a touch, and I need more but he won't give it to me. Instead, he just stares down at me with hungry eyes.

"My house, tonight. You be there, or I come and find you. Don't think I'm fuckin' kidding, Addison. Be there."

"I don't even know where you live," I retort.

"You do, babe, 'coz I fucked you on the bike right outside my front door."

Ohhhh, so that was his house. Thank God for that.

I swallow, licking my bottom lip. He doesn't give me a chance to argue any further. He lets me go and moves away before I can take my next breath. I stare at the empty space a moment longer, before letting out a rude snort. Cade Duke is going to see that he doesn't get to order me around.

I won't be at his house tonight.

Let's see how he takes that.

~*CHAPTER 8*~

PAST

"Addison, baby, you're killing me."

I smile up at Billy. He reaches over, takes my hair in his fingers and twirls it. We're driving, and for the first time in years, I feel completely at ease. I run my fingers up his thigh. When you're nineteen years old – which we both are – that's an extremely sexual gesture. He's all stiff and squirming, begging me to stop teasing him. I'm giggling. I almost forgot what giggling felt like.

"I'm not doing anything," I smile innocently.

He grins, flashing me his charming, crooked smile. His blonde hair blows in the wind and his eyes twinkle with amusement.

"I won't be able to drop you off if you keep that up."

I frown now. "I wish you didn't have to drop me off."

He gives me a pained smile. "I know, baby, but for now I can't keep you. I have to get a place first."

I nod, knowing that's the truth. He's trying. He's trying to get out of his parents' house and find a way to save me. I'm sure he will too. At least, I hope he will. Right now, he's my light at the end of the tunnel. If that light snuffs out, I really don't think I'll find another one.

"We'll be fine," he assures me as he turns onto my street.

My heart sinks, that quickly. There's nothing but darkness here.

"Thanks, for today," I whisper as Billy comes to a stop.

He reaches over taking my face in his hands. "I'll find a way to save you, Addison. I swear."

I lean over and brush my lips across his. He tangles his fingers in my hair and deepens the kiss. Finally, we break apart, my heart thudding. He strokes a thumb down my cheek.

"I'll call you, I promise."

"The phone has been disconnected again," I sigh.

He keeps his smile, even though I see he wants to frown.

"Well, I'll come by and see you tomorrow."

I kiss him goodbye, and with a heavy heart, I walk up my front steps. When I get to the rickety front door, I turn back and stare at Billy's car disappearing down the street. I give it a sad smile, and step inside. The first thing I smell is vomit, then I see my mother on the floor, choking on her own sick, her face turning blue as her she struggles to breathe. She's too high, too floppy, and incapable of stopping her own vomit from choking her. With a sigh, and a slump of my shoulders, I get to work doing what I do best.

Looking after a woman I despise, because she's all I have.

That's what I like to call tragic.

~*PRESENT*~

It's dark when I leave the compound, and it's late. I finished work earlier, but I spent a bit of time with Jackson. Surprisingly, we had a decent conversation. I may have also been avoiding running into Cade. I know he went home hours ago. I also know I was meant to be there hours ago. So, here I am, walking down the dark road on my own. It's really not safe, but I'm used to it. It's getting cool, and a light breeze tickles my face. I hear the rumbling sound of a truck coming in my direction, so I step off the road a little further. When the truck stops, I turn to see why. My heart begins to thump, an instant reaction to a strange truck pulling over at this time of the night.

The truck engine stops, so I quickly begin walking again at a more rapid pace. I dig about for my phone just in case I need to run and call someone at the same time. I hear the truck door slam, and a set of heavy boots striding at a rapid pace towards me. I spin around, throwing my hands up. "Back up!"

"What the fuck are you doin' walkin' around at night on your own? I thought you had a fuckin' lift!"

It's Cade. Of course it is.

"I'm going home," I say, breathing heavily to try and steady my thumping heart.

"Pardon?" he says, his voice rough.

"You heard me, I'm going home. You can't just order me over to your house Cade, it doesn't work like that."

"Yeah, babe, it fuckin' does."

I glare at him. I can just see him in the light.

"No, babe, it fuckin' doesn't," I mock, turning.

"Addison, I'll toss you in that fuckin' truck. Don't make me use force."

I gape and turn back. "Are you serious? You can't force me to go with you."

"It wouldn't be force if you just accepted you want me as much as I fuckin' want you."

"You've lost it, you know that?"

"Three seconds to get in the truck."

"You are insane…"

"Three."

"Fuck you, Cade."

"Two."

"I'm not going with you!"

"One."

He steps forward, drops his shoulder and lifts me up in one motion. I squeal and pound my fists on his back, but he simply keeps striding towards his truck. He opens the door and throws me in, then, through my squirming, he also manages to buckles me in. Before he closes the door, he leans down close, "Don't even think about tryin' to get out, or I'll tie you to the fuckin' chair."

My mouth drops open as he closes the door and walks around the driver's side, gets in and slams the door. What kind of biker drives a truck anyway? I cross my arms and stare out the window as he pulls onto the highway.

"I'm not fucking you. You're wasting your time."

He snorts. "Sugar, my cock is goin' inside you tonight and you know it. You also know I'm not wasting my time, because you and I both know, you could have fought me off if you really wanted to."

Damn him.

"You're a frustrating, intense man, do you hear me?" I say, turning to stare at him.

In the moonlight, his profile looks dazzling. Strong, square jaw. Perfect Roman nose and full lips. He's divine.

"Yeah, sugar, I'm hearin' ya."

My lips twitch and he looks at me from the corner of his eye. He grins, and my heart throbs.

"You're gonna smile for me tonight, baby. I'll make sure of it."

I turn and stare out the window, because what he doesn't know, is that I'm already smiling.

~*CHAPTER 9*~

PRESENT

Cade's house, is totally not what I expected a man like him to have. The large, pretty white home is quite enchanting. When we get out of the truck and walk inside, I am in awe. It's massive, with polished wooden floors, white timber walls and some seriously nice furniture. It is, without a doubt, the nicest house I've ever seen. I stare around, mouth open, completely lost for words. Cade walks up behind me, sweeps my hair off my neck and trails his lips over the back. I feel my body begin to quake, and I stare down at his hands sliding around my waist.

"The look on your face right now, it makes my heart hurt, sugar."

I swallow down my emotions and turn to face him. Right now, I don't want to fight him. Him bringing me here, and pushing me even when I fought him, that tells me that to him, I am so much more than just sex. He's a hard man; there's no doubt about that, and being with him wouldn't be easy. I don't even know if being with him is something that I should be doing, but right now, in this moment, I'm okay with doing it.

"Saying sweet things doesn't suit you, biker," I say in a small voice.

He chuckles. "Yeah, got ya. I'll go back to being an ass."

My lips twitch again, and he stares down at them. "I'll get that smile, sugar. Now, have you eaten?"

I feel my eyes widen and he snorts, shrugging off his leather jacket.

"What? Don't think a biker can cook?"

I put my hands up in defense. "Hey, I didn't say that."

"No, spose' you didn't. Now, have you eaten?"

84

I shake my head, eating isn't something I do a lot of. Habit I guess. That's what happens when you don't have a great deal of food offered during your life.

"Right, we're goin' to cook somethin' up, then I'm goin' to fuck you until you're screamin' my name."

My brows shoot up. "I love how you assume you're that good."

He leans in close, sliding his tongue across my bottom lip. "I am that good, sugar, and you know it."

I bite his tongue. He grunts, wraps his arms around my waist and presses against me. He tilts his head, pushes forward, and turns his licking into a deep kiss that has my entire body sparking to life. I hook my fingers through the loops on his jeans and pull his hips against my pelvis, enjoying the feeling of his hard cock riding against me.

"I may have a few tricks up my sleeve to make you squeal," I murmur, sliding my hand around to rub against his cock.

He makes a purring sound and leans down to nip my earlobe. "Bring it on. Ain't nothin' you do, is gonna make me squeal."

I grin at him. "Is that a challenge, biker?"

He slaps my ass and then lets me go. "It most certainly is a challenge."

"Well consider it accepted!" I call after him as he makes his way into the large kitchen.

"Well consider me fuckin' thrilled."

I am beaming inside as I follow him into the large kitchen with white counter tops and stainless steel appliances. I grip the counter and lift myself until I'm sitting on it. I watch Cade dig through the fridge to come out with a mass of ingredients. Many men say they can cook.

Whether it actually tastes good or not, is to be decided upon serving. My guess, Cade can cook.

"You just gonna sit there and watch?" he says, throwing some steak down onto a cutting board.

"It's proper manners to cook for a lady, you know."

"Ain't got manners, and there ain't no lady here."

I thump his shoulder and he chuckles.

"So, is this your common wooing technique?"

He looks up at me mid-way through trimming the fat off the steak.

"One, sugar, I don't woo women. I don't have to. Two, do I look like the type to woo, even if I had to? Three, you're the first girl I've cooked for in at least five years."

"How old are you, gramps?"

He shakes his head, but I can see a ghost of a smile playing around his mouth. "I'm twenty-nine."

I feel my expression change to one of shock. I knew Cade was older than me, but I didn't realize he was eight years old than me.

"Too old for you?" he murmurs when he notices my expression.

"No, why would you think that?"

"You're giving me a horrified expression."

Change of subject, Addison.

"I just think you're young to be a vice president of a MC club. That's a big thing."

He shrugs. "Not for me."

"Why'd you join?"

He pulls out a potato and begins peeling it. "Jack's helped me. I was in a bad place and he pulled me from it. We got close, he trusted me, so he gave me the role two years ago."

"My dad is the reason?"

He nods, giving me a quick glance. "Shocked by that?"

"A little, but I guess I can understand it."

"He changed my world. He dragged me from a shitty place."

I cross my legs, press my palms to the counter and lean forward. "What sort of bad place?"

"Drugs, sex, crime…guilt."

"Guilt?"

He stiffens a touch, and I notice it. What is Cade hiding? What did he do that would make him feel enough guilt that he can't even say the word without stiffening? Is that why he's so determined to be with me? Can he see himself in me? Or is he trying to fix me because he couldn't fix himself? Humans are like that sometimes, they seek something to put back together when they're broken and can't fix themselves. I guess it's just a comfort; it makes us feel better, like we haven't completely lost ourselves – we like to believe there's still a part in there, that can be saved.

"That's a story I ain't willin' to tell."

I nod, completely understanding. I am not ready to tell my story either. And boy, do I have a story to tell.

"I understand that."

He stops peeling the potato and looks up. "That ain't the reaction I expected."

"What reaction did you think you would get?"

"Most girls roll their eyes and pout, or try to soothe me with words that mean sweet fuck all to me."

I shrug, meeting his gaze. "I've been in a place I don't really want to share with the world. I know what it's like to have a story you don't want to tell. Not all stories have to be told, you know, sometimes…sometimes they are better left closed."

He stares at me a long moment, his gaze deep. "Ain't ever heard it put that way, but sugar, I like it."

I nod, looking down. He drops what he's doing, walks over and lifts my chin until my eyes meet his.

"I know what you went through was all kinds of fucked up, and one day maybe you'll tell me about it, just like maybe I'll tell you. If you wanna tell me bits, the lot, or none, that's up to you. I ain't ever gonna push, just like I'm never gonna judge. Your life was bad; I see it in your eyes. When you grin, your face is empty, and I have no doubt when you smile, your eyes won't shine like they should. One day though, baby, I will make them shine."

I swallow, and I do something I have never done in my life, I reach out for him. I take his face, stroke my thumb over his lip ring, then I lean down and I kiss him. It's soft, gentle and there's something behind it I am so afraid to face. If I face it, then I have to face what I'm running from. If I face that, then I know things are going to change for me in big ways. I pull back, and Cade locks eyes with me for the longest moment, before he turns back towards his preparation. Taking a deep breath, I decide it's time to change the subject and steer it away from this emotional stuff; it's too much to process right now.

"So, Britney…where does she fit in all this?"

He grunts, shaking his head. "She's a fuckin' pain in the ass."

"Why do you sleep with her?"

"Haven't fucked her since you showed up."

This surprises me. It truly does. "Why?"

"You know why, sugar. Don't make me do sappy – I can say nice shit, but I don't do sappy."

"Okay, so you stopped fucking her to fuck me. Why is she so convinced she's the only one you go back to?"

"Because she was for a long time."

"Oh, you two were together?"

Makes a little more sense now.

"Not exactly. She came in with one of the other guys. It didn't work out, so she became a drifter. She slept around with the members, worked the bar, wormed her way into the club and that's when she took a liking to me. Britney's a wild fuck, so I spent a bit of time with her. She became a regular fuck. I know what you think of me, sugar, you think I get around and I won't lie and say I haven't, but I prefer one constant. Britney was that for a long time, over three years to be precise, but she got on my nerves. She started pushing to be my old lady, and there was no way in fuck that was happening, so I dropped her. I still fucked her, but no way near as frequently."

"Oh, okay…well then…"

He grins. "Shocked, babe?"

"No, it's exactly how I pinned your relationship with her. She's quite determined to be the only woman you have in your life."

"Well, she don't get to make that choice for me. Watch out for her, yeah?"

I wave my hand. "Seriously? Britney? Not worried at all."

"Sugar, she don't play nice. Watch out for her."

"I'm fine."

"Babe…"

"Cade…"

"You'll be careful, yeah?"

I sigh in defeat. "Yeah, I'll be careful."

"I know you're just sayin' that so I'll shut up, but fine, it'll do for now."

I grin at him and he returns it with full force before returning to his cooking. I watch him for the next hour, preparing and creating. He makes steak, with baked potatoes stuffed with a creamy-cheese mix and a garden salad. We sit down with a beer, and eat in silence. The food is that divine, we don't need to speak. When we're done, I gather the plates and take them to the sink and begin cleaning up. When I notice Cade leaning against the counter watching me, I stop, turn, and put my hands on my hips.

"You gonna help me?"

"No sugar."

"Fine, then I'm not doing them!"

"Ain't it a woman's job?"

My eyes widen and I grip the dish towel, lunging at him. He grins and side steps me, but I manage to crack the towel and it hits his belly. He grunts in pain and dives for me, hits my belly with his shoulder and lifts me up. He brings his hand down over my ass and I squeal, giggling. He turns, striding towards the stairs.

"What about the cleaning up?" I laugh.

"Fuck the cleaning up. I'm going to spend the rest of the night deep in your sweet pussy."

Well, how can a girl argue with that?

91

~*CHAPTER 10*~

PRESENT

My back hits Cade's soft mattress and I make a whimpering sound. Cade stands back, staring down at me; his eyes hooded, his body stiff and ready. His tongue snakes out and licks his bottom lip as he grips his shirt. He lifts the hem and takes it over his head. When he shows me his broad, hairless chest, I tremble. I get a good look at the tattoos under this light, and I can't help but lick my lips. He's got 'Hell's Knights' tattooed in a curved style on his chest. He's also got a star-like creation on his ripped belly. Just under his belly button, he has the words 'Every second counts'. I feel my eyes grow heavy as I let my gaze slowly rake over him.

He grips his jeans and lowers them slowly, as though he's teasing me. I slide my hand up my shirt, and tweak my already hardening nipple. One thing I do know how to do is pleasure myself. I've seen every possible sexual act there is, and I know how to make everything feel better. Cade watches my hand, and his breathing deepens. When his jeans hit the floor, I let my eyes drop to his erect cock. Sweet mother, it's beautiful. Standing tall, pierced through the head, and thick as hell. He wraps his fingers around it and begins stoking. His hand moves with perfect rhythm. I swallow, grip my shirt and bring it up over my head. I unclip my bra and toss it off. Cade growls and crawls onto the bed.

"Straddle my chest," I whisper.

His eyes widen a little. "Why?" he rasps.

"Trust me. Do it."

He puts his legs either side of me and rests on his knees, then he shuffles up until he's over my waist. His cock juts out proudly right near my mouth. I snake my tongue out and lick the head. Cade hisses and squeezes the base of his dick, stroking in short, hard bursts. I slide my fingers up his sides and he flinches. I use just enough nail to give him a hint of pain. Men like that. They also like things near their ass. I don't know how Cade will take what I have planned, but I'm about to find out.

"Keep stroking," I rasp.

"Fuck. I love how fuckin' dirty you are."

I grin up at him, then I lean forward a little and put a pillow under my head. Then I take his cock into my mouth, only sucking the head. I swirl my tongue around the tip, tasting him, enjoying the moment. His grunts spur me on, and his hand moves a little harder, a little faster, as he picks up his pace. I swirl my tongue around the barbell in his head, then I tug it lightly with my teeth. He groans deeply and his chest tightens, causing his muscles to bunch. Holy shit, that's a gorgeous chest. I slide my fingers beneath his cock, cup his balls and roll them in my hands. He growls at me, and I give his head a little nip with my teeth.

"Mother fucker," he snarls. "I'll come before I fuck you, sugar, if you don't stop."

I don't stop, I clench my teeth down harder around him and tease him with my tongue. My fingers tickle his heavy sack, and when I feel the swell of his cock in my mouth, I know he's ready to come. That's when I slide one finger into his ass. Her jerks so violently, completely shocked. I tilt my finger, finding the tiny sweet spot all men have. The first spurt of his release doesn't shock me; I have read how hard this makes a man come. His roaring and the way he clenches the sheets beside him, his head thrown back, his chest heaving, tells me that the stories are true; it does make it more mind blowing for a man. I press again and he spurts once more, filling my mouth.

"Fuck! Holy fuck!" he groans.

When he stops pulsing, and his erection begins to die down, I remove my mouth and my finger, and I look up at him. He stares down at me, completely shocked and content.

"The fuck?" he says in a scratchy voice. His dark hair falls over his face, making him look completely dangerous and yet so young at the same time.

"I told you I could make you squeal," I smile.

His face lights up, and he leans down grazing my head with his lips. "I told you I could make you smile. Guess we were both right, yeah?"

"Yeah," I chuckle.

"Give me ten, sugar. I'll be deep inside you…"

I flush and shift. Cade gets off me and falls down onto his back. We both stare at the ceiling for a long moment, both of us no doubt feeling the same rush of emotions. Cade fits me. There's just something about him that fits. He molds into me in a way no one has before. It both frightens and thrills me. I roll towards him, sliding my fingers across his chest. He looks at me, his eyes intense.

"Somethin' about you, sugar, it's makin' everything I believed in feel like it never existed."

"Yeah," I whisper. "I'm feeling it too, but don't go getting all sappy on me, biker."

He gives me a heated expression, then he rolls, dropping his mouth to my nipple. He closes it over the hard tip, sucks and gives it a flick with his tongue every now and then. I moan and let my head sink into the pillow. While his mouth is on my nipple, his hand gently massages my other breast. I whimper, never having felt so many bolts of pleasure shooting through my body just from nipple stimulation.

"Cade," I whisper. "God, more."

He lets his hand slide from my breast and he slides it down to my pants. He tugs at them, and I let him pull them off. When I'm in nothing but my panties, I feel my body begin to liven up again. He cups my pussy, pressing his palm into my damp mound.

"Fuckin' wet, God, sugar, need my cock inside you, but not until I taste that sweet cunt again."

I tremble as he grips my panties and tears them off in one, quick swipe. When I am exposed to him, he leans back and takes hold of my knees, spreading them.

"You're shining for me, baby, so fuckin' wet. Show me how you like it."

I look up at him, and he's giving me an expression that has my heart thudding.

"You want me to touch myself?"

"Yeah, babe, fuck…yeah."

I slide my fingers down my belly, and when I reach my pussy, I slide my finger through my folds. Cade swallows and watches as I lift my finger out and bring it to my lips.

"Jesus fucking Christ," he rasps.

I stretch my finger out, and he leans forward, taking it into his mouth and sucking. The feeling of having someone suck your finger is fucking erotic. I clench, desperately needing attention. When my finger slips from his mouth, he gently takes my hands, placing them above my head.

"I'm going to make you come now, sugar, so keep your hands up there."

I spread my legs further as he leans down. He takes hold of my hips and tilts them upwards. When his mouth closes over my pussy, the cry that escapes my throat is strangled and raw. He sucks my clit into his mouth, gently rotating it around and around until I'm wound up so tightly it almost hurts.

"Cade, please," I beg, thrashing in his grips.

He slips a finger inside me, then two, and before I can think, he's thrusting and sucking, thrusting and sucking. When I come, it's out of this world. I shake, twist, cry out and jerk until every last jolt of pleasure has been wrung from my body. Cade crawls up over me, reaches over to the bedside table and pulls out a condom. He sits back and I watch as he slides it down his hard length. When he's fully sheathed, he positions himself over me and wraps my legs around his hips before pressing against my entrance. I groan as he stretches and fills me with each gentle push inside.

"Fuck, Cade!"

"Sugar," he groans, "you're fuckin' killin' me."

He slips deep inside, and the feeling of him filling me is so intense, I close my eyes and just enjoy the moment. Cade thrusts his hips, slides out and fills me again. His elbows rest beside my head, so I turn my head to the left and lick his biceps. He groans and tangles a hand in my hair, tugging gently. I whimper as I begin to swell around him; he's tweaking the perfect spots inside me.

"Need you deeper," he growls gripping my hips and rolling us.

We roll too far, and end up off the bed and thumping down onto the floor. I squeal, he laughs. The idea of moving only crosses my mind for a split second, but instead, I crush my lips against Cade's and then we're fucking like wild animals. The carpet rug is burning my back as I use the bed to press my feet against, so my legs are high and raised. Cade drives me hard, his fingers are tangled in my hair;

our bodies are sweaty and we both heave and pant, our groans join together to make a primal, feral sound.

"Fuck, goin' to come," Cade rasps. "Come with me."

I am gripping his back so hard I can feel warmth on my fingers. He grunts loudly as I drag my nails down his skin. I'm so close, God, I'm so close. Cade reaches between us and tweaks my clit, and that sends me over the edge. With a scream, I come. Cade is close behind me, and his primal bellow completely increases my release. We shudder together. My back burns; my body is on fire and I love it. I love every second of it. When his orgasm dies down, he drops his head into my shoulder, kissing it gently. He rolls us both to our sides, until we're facing each other.

"Fuck, you got some nails, girl," he murmurs. "My back hurts."

"Mine too," I groan, shifting.

"What's wrong with yours?" he says, moving a piece of hair from my eyes.

"Carpet burn."

He stares blankly at me, then bursts out laughing. I shove at his chest, but he grips my wrists and pulls me close.

"Sorry, baby, that was so unexpected."

"I can't believe we rolled off the bed."

He grins, kissing me softly. "Wild cat."

"Rebel."

He sits us up, and then his hands are on me, gently, spinning me around. He runs his fingertips over my battered back. He leans in, kissing it softly, completely shocking me. To the rest of the world, Cade is terrifying, but here…in this moment…he's completely beautiful.

"Let me get somethin' to put on that."

He stands, takes my hands and helps me up. My body aches in the most pleasant way; it's a thrilling feeling. It's a feeling I've never had before.

And it scares the hell out of me.

~*CHAPTER 11*~

PAST

"I tried to call you," I say, when Billy finally comes around after four days of me desperately trying to contact him.

"I was busy," he says, but his voice sounds off.

He's sounded off for weeks. It's almost like he doesn't want to be here, but he's too afraid to tell me so. He's trying to save me, and I'm starting to feel more and more like a project than I am a girlfriend. He runs his fingers through his messy blonde hair and sighs. "Listen, Addison, we need to-"

"Don't bother," I snap, crossing my arms. "I know what you're going to say."

He does look like it pains him to have to say what comes next, and that only makes my heart hurt more. I don't doubt Billy cares about me, but I think it's gone far beyond that. Sometimes caring just isn't enough, and sometimes one's lifestyle is unfixable. Perhaps that's how he feels about my lifestyle, that I'll never leave it, never get away. I swallow and square my shoulders. I've dealt with far worse than heart break. I don't expect Billy to save me. How can I ever expect someone to change their world for me? That's such a high expectation to have of another person, especially when what they're fighting for, is completely fucked up to begin with.

"You know I love you, Addison," he says gently.

I hate that line. You know I love you, but I'm going to leave you anyway. I thought love conquered all? Seems to me, if things get too hard, people run regardless of love. Whatever happened to through thick and thin? I don't let Billy see the hurt that's ripping through my chest right now. I won't be the girl that begs. I've never been that girl and I won't start now.

"You're leaving," I respond in a simple, emotionless tone.

Billy flinches, and I see his fingers twitching like he wants to reach out for me. He makes a loud, sighing sound and begins pacing the room.

"It's work."

What a fucking lie.

"No, it's not."

He stops pacing and turns to face me. He shoves his hands into his jean pockets.

"Addison, it's just...look...I want a certain lifestyle and you're not willing to walk away from this to be with me. I can't keep trying to save a girl, who doesn't want to be saved."

"You think it's so easy, don't you?" I snap.

"No, I don't think it's easy. I've seen how hard it is for you. I know what you go through here but you won't let me help you. You won't walk away from her. You won't walk away from Jasper, even after..."

His face scrunches in disgust, and that burns. It burns because that disgust isn't just because of Jasper, it's because of me. Because I allow it, because I stopped fighting.

"He hurts you, and you let him. Your mother treats you like a dog, and you let her. You won't walk away because you're scared if you do and we don't work out, that you'll have nothing."

This hurts me. He has no idea how it is for me. I can't walk away from this, because if I do, it could so easily backfire. If I step away from my mother, she won't ever take me back. If it doesn't work out with Billy, where does that leave me? Being forced to live like her? Being forced to sleep around to earn money? I have no skills. No one will take scum like me. It's so easy for him to see the light at the end of the tunnel because he's never had to walk in darkness.

"Have you ever spent a night on the streets, Billy?"

He scrunches up his face. "You know I haven't."

"Then you couldn't begin to imagine how terrible it is. I would do anything to avoid ever having to go there again. You don't understand my resistance, because you haven't had to live the way I do."

"If you would just trust me…"

"Trust isn't the problem. The problem is that if you leave me, I have nothing."

"You're worrying about something that may never happen, Addison."

"I have to protect myself, and if you're not willing to wait…"

"I've waited over six months!" he yells. "How much longer do you need?"

I shake my head, swallowing down my emotions. "Never mind, Billy, do what you have to do."

"Addison, this isn't what I want, but your life is holding me back…"

I stare down at my hands and my eyes burn; they burn so badly I struggle to keep them open.

"Thanks for everything, Billy," I whisper.

"Addison…"

"Please leave. If you're going to leave, then walk out now because I can't handle you standing here trying to make me feel better about the fact that you're giving up on me."

"God, Addison…"

"Leave."

He does. He turns, walks to the door and only stops to whisper another sorry before he steps out. When he's gone, the hot tears slip down my cheeks. My small chance of freedom just walked away from me, and there's not a damned thing I can do to stop him. Not a single thing. I wrap my arms around my legs and rock backwards and forwards, fighting every part in me that screams to go after him. I can't go after him. I know I can't. Billy made it clear he's not willing to fight. It's just me now – I am all that I have left. How utterly pitiful.

"Well, well."

I hear Jasper's creepy voice, and snap my head up. He's standing at the door Billy walked out of only five minutes earlier. He's smiling, and it makes my stomach turn.

"Such a shame," he purrs. "I thought he was a keeper."

My blood goes cold. How did he know? Was he listening? Did he just stand there and wait for Billy to leave before he came in? I keep my hands firmly wrapped around my knees, not willing to move. Jasper walks in, running his fingers over the old mattered couch. I shudder, and not in a good way.

"What are we going to do now he's gone?"

I swallow. For six month's I've been free of Jasper. The idea of him touching me again makes me feel sick inside.

"Get lost," I breathe. "I'll call him and he'll come back."

Jasper throws his head back and laughs. "For scum like you? Oh snake, I don't think so."

"Just stay away from me!"

He grips his belt and begins undoing it.

"See, that's not going to happen and you know it. You owe me."

I close my eyes and pray that he dies right now of a heart attack, a stroke, anything. Anything to keep his filthy hands off me. I begin sobbing, which is so unlike me. I don't sob. I don't cry, I just go with everything that's thrown at me. I don't want to live in this nightmare anymore. There's nothing left for me, nothing but darkness and pain. I shift off the couch, feeling my world spin as I back around behind it. Jasper continues to walk toward me, grinning. I reach into my bag and I pull out the pills my mother left behind this morning. I don't know what they are, ecstasy maybe.

"That's right snake, you know you can't escape me."

I pour all of them onto my hand, and I throw them into my mouth and swallow. Jasper's eyes widen, and he lunges forward. I spin around, run into the bathroom, slam the door and lock it. I rush to the sink, lean over and swallow loads of water to make the process quicker. Then, I sink to the floor, hot tears pouring from my eyes.

"Open the door!" Jasper roars, pounding heavily with his fists.

I put my head in my hands and wait for darkness to win. I just want away from this pain. I'll never be free of it. I honestly can't think about anything but the gripping pain wrapping itself around my heart. There's no escape, no matter which way I run. My only chance of survival is gone, and without even a ray of sunshine in my life, I've got nothing to hold onto. This is the only way.

The only way to find my light at the end of this long, dark tunnel.

~*PRESENT*~

"What happened to the man?"

I'm lying in Cade's bed, my eyes heavy and my body relaxed.

"What man?" I ask, running my fingers up and down his taut arms.

103

"You said the other day that you've only been with a few men, one of them saved you."

I swallow and turn my face up towards the ceiling.

"He left me."

Cade's quiet a moment.

"Then he's a cunt."

I snort a laugh, and roll towards him. He rolls too, and we adjust ourselves so we're face to face, hands tangled together.

"That's one way of putting it."

"He left 'coz your life was too hard, yeah?"

I nod, avoiding his gaze. He reaches up between us and grips my chin, forcing me to look back at him. "That's a coward's way out, you know that?"

"Yeah," I whisper.

"Little prick broke part of you though, didn't he?"

"He made me stop believing."

Cade's eyes scan my face, and his mouth tightens. "No one ever has the right to take that away from another person."

"He was all I had. He stopped the rape. He made me think I had a way out. He didn't want to wait. He didn't understand that I couldn't just leave the situation I was in. What if it didn't work out? My mother would have never taken me back."

"Men with nice lives will never understand what it's like to live with nothing."

"No," I say simply. "They won't."

"So he left, and then your ma died?"

"A few months later, yeah."

"Then you ran?"

"I left," I correct him, but I hear the lie in my voice.

"Lyin', babe."

"Stop telling me I'm lying; you don't know my story, Cade."

"No," he says, rolling to his back. "I don't know your story, but I can see the fear in your eyes."

"You see years and years of bad things in my eyes. It's not fear."

"It is fear."

"No, it's not."

He rolls again and grips my chin. "Sugar, it is."

I jerk my chin from his grip and roll off the bed. I get to my feet and yank on my top.

"Don't go runnin' 'coz I raised somethin' you're tryin' to hide."

I glare at him. "I'm going home because I'm tired."

He puts his hands behind his head and stares over at me. "You always run when things go bad?"

My anger is boiling inside of me. "Whatever, Cade, I'm going. Thanks for tonight."

"You wanna leave in a hiss, go ahead. I ain't chasin' ya, sugar. It ain't how I roll. You wanna get into the bed; I'll talk to you. I'll fuck you again and I'll even hold you while you sleep, but if you wanna storm out, I'm not comin' after you. I don't play with women. If they want the good side of me, they get in and let me give it, but if they wanna run out in a mood, that ain't my issue."

I pick up my purse and then turn to stare at him. "I don't want or need you to chase me, Cade."

Then I turn and walk out of the room. When I'm out the front door and walking down the road, my chest seizes because part of me, deep down, wanted him to chase me.

~*CHAPTER 12*~

PRESENT

I hear the rumble of a mass of Harley Davidson's as I near Jackson's house. I know it's not Cade, because he's not likely to be riding in a group only ten minutes after I left him naked in a bed. I turn and stare as the mass of headlights coming up and over the hill. I squint my eyes wondering if it's Jackson heading home or out on a ride with the guys. When the bikes begin to slow down, I notice right away that it isn't the Hell's Knights. It's another group and my body instantly seizes with panic. I take a few steps back, now understanding why walking home is not safe. I have no chance against this many bikers.

When the bikes come to a stop, the man in front on a dark black Fat Boy, gets off his bike and pulls off his helmet. I feel my eyes widen at the sight of him. He's gorgeous, no, he's beyond gorgeous. He's to die for. He's very different to Cade. While Cade is dark, dangerous and completely sexy – this man has lighter hair, darker eyes, but is just as completely terrifying to look at. His boots crunch in the dried up leaves on the road as he walks closer to me. When he stops in front of me, I see his eyes are so brown they nearly look black. He has sandy blonde hair that's ruffled and he is covered in tattoos. I swallow, but square my shoulders. Maybe they're friends of Jackson's?

"Let me guess," the biker purrs, his voice is rough, husky and very attractive. "You must be Jacks' little girl?"

"I'm nobody's little girl," I say back, though my voice doesn't come out as strong as I'd like.

Blondie chuckles and crosses his arms. He's broad, not as tall as Cade but thicker across the shoulders.

"Heard all about you. I thought you would be a little more difficult to find though."

I shake my head. "What are you talking about?"

He grins, showing me one perfect dimple. "Are you familiar with a man named Jasper?"

I flinch and he chuckles. "Thought so. See, I heard you left a bit of a mess behind and Jasper wasn't very happy about it. So, he hired me. See, I'm a fantastic tracker, and he didn't want to get his hands dirty. If he came after you, he was riskin' too much, so here I am."

I feel my hands shaking, but I clench them together. God, why did I leave Cade? Me and my stubborn mind.

"I did nothing to Jasper," I say, my voice not as strong as it should be.

"Oh precious, we both know that's a lie."

"What do you want? To tell him where I am? Go ahead, I'll run."

The man laughs. "I'll just find you. It wasn't hard to do the first time; it won't be again."

"You found me because of my last name and the fact that my father is a biker. Do you think I'm stupid? You knew where to look, Jasper didn't, so he sent a biker knowing he'd find another biker easily."

Blondie's face flinches, but I continue. "So go ahead, tell him. I'm only going to run."

I take a step back, pull out my phone and press the speed dial to Cade. I put it in at the store the other day in case he decided he didn't want to wait around for me and I needed to find him. Thank God for that.

"Who you callin', precious? Daddy? He can't help you."

"I'm calling my...um...boyfriend, Cade."

God, did I just say that? I sound so...childish. I do notice Blondie flinch at the mention of Cade's name though, and that sparks my interest.

"Say again?" he rasps, his voice thick.

So he does know Cade? That's interesting.

"He won't be happy about this," I attempt. "He's part of my father's club, and when the guys show up..."

"That's where the little fuck went," Blondie grunts, cutting me off.

"Sugar?" I hear in my ear as Cade answers the phone. "Did ya change your mind?"

"Cade, there's this man and..."

Blondie smirks, then leans forward and snatches the phone from my hand and presses it to his ear.

"Cade, long time no see, brother."

I hope he means that in the non-literal sense.

"Yeah, it's Spike. Don't sound so shocked, you didn't think you'd never see me again, did you?"

What the hell is going down between these two?

"Oh, we'll be waiting for you. By all means, bring your club. We'd love to tango."

That doesn't sound good.

Spike hangs up the phone and grins at me. "Well, well, you just made it all the more interesting. I've been looking to catch up with Cade for a long time."

I cross my arms rubbing them. I have to get out of here. I have to escape while Cade distracts them. Provided Cade doesn't show up, guns blaring. Then I won't be able to run. It's just not in me. I hope he shows up alone and whisks me away. I look over Spike's shoulder at the six or so bikes still rumbling on the side of the road. At least, he doesn't have all his guys with him, or maybe that is all of them. I can only hope so. I let my eyes fall on Spike's again. I'm still shocked Jasper would contact a biker gang to locate me. That's so...weak.

"Cade's not going to let you share my location," I say in a snarky voice.

"He can't stop me, precious," Spike grins. "And trust me when I say, I don't owe him nothin'."

"Just leave me be, Jasper asked for everything he got. I'm not doing anything wrong. I just want to start again."

Spike shrugs. "Never said he didn't ask for it. He pays me. I deliver. It's that simple. No offence to you, precious."

"No offence to me?" I growl. "You're happy handing me back to a man who raped me my entire life?"

Spike jerks and his eyes widen. "What?"

"Some man you are."

I hear the rumble of Harley's and I see about ten of them come over the rise. Shit! Cade isn't slow. I know most of the bikers would have been at the compound which is only a minute away, but still. He must have frantically made some calls. When the bikes slow down, I see that Jackson is up the front and Cade is behind him. They are the only two that get off, the others just idle away, like Spike's guys are doing. The two men walk towards me, and I feel a mild amount of relief. I feel Cade's fingers wrap around my wrist and hurl me backwards. I want to tuck myself into him and not move. He feels safe.

110

"Well, hello, old friend," Spike murmurs, stepping closer.

"Spike," Cade says simply.

There's a lot of shit going down between these two; I can see it in their eyes. My guess? These two were once great friends and something bad happened. Maybe that's what Cade didn't want to talk about? I press myself further into Cade's side, and I see Jackson give us a quick, curious glance before stepping closer to Spike.

"Why are you here, Spike?"

"Good to see you too, Jacks."

Jackson crosses his large arms. "Don't play with me, boy. I've been kickin' your ass my entire life and I'll do it again. You know my boys will have yours out of this town in a mother fuckin' second."

My father has known Spike that long?

Spike narrows his eyes, then turns his gaze to me. "I've come to do what I had to do, though I will be stayin' a week or so. Got a trip planned, need to stock up on supplies."

"You can do whatever you want. I don't own the town, but if you cause shit, I'll finish you," Jackson warns.

"The fuck did you come here to sort?" Cade snaps, not letting Spike answer Jackson's threat.

Spike keeps his eyes on me for a moment. I'm sure I see that he's unsure about what he's doing. He quickly covers it though. "Your girl here, is a wanted one..."

Cade flinches. "What?"

"I was paid to track her."

Jackson turns and stares at me, his eyes confused.

"What for?" he asks me.

"It's a long story."

"You being followed, and you didn't think to fuckin' mention that?" Cade barks.

I flinch and attempt to step out of his grips, but he holds me close. "Don't fuckin' move," he snarls to me, then he turns to Spike. "Get the fuck outta town, Spike. You ain't reportin' shit to anyone."

"Been paid good dollars to report her location," Spike says, glaring at Cade.

"I'll double it. Just keep the fuck away from my girl."

His girl? What the hell? Both Jackson and Spike raise their brows.

"What the fuck?" Jackson snarls.

"You wanna pay me double, not to tell that pimp cunt that she's here?" Spike says, shaking his head a little, completely ignoring Jackson's outburst.

Cade's voice comes out like ice. "That's what I fuckin' said."

"You in love with her, Duke?"

Cade flinches. "She's mine. I protect what's mine."

Spike's face turns bitter. "Pity you don't protect what's not yours."

"Not now," Cade warns.

"Oh, touchy subject, Cade?"

What the hell are they talking about now?

"You gonna get outta town, or do I need to end this now?" Cade grinds out.

"I'm stayin', your boss man just told me I was. You pay me and I'll tell the man the girl is gone."

I slump in relief.

"Give me a number," Cade hisses.

"Cade..." I start to say, but the look he shoots down at me is enough to make me shut my mouth.

"Fifty thousand."

Fifty thousand dollars! My mouth drops open. That means Jasper paid Spike twenty-five-thousand dollars just to find me. My body begins feeling cold.

"Done. I'll wire it."

"Cade you can't," I protest.

"Shut the fuck up, sugar."

"But..."

"Now," he orders.

I close my mouth, but guilt fills me. What if Cade doesn't have that kind of money? Spike watches us a moment, then cracks his neck from side to side.

"You got twenty-four hours, Duke. You don't wire it, I give her location." With that, he turns and walks back towards his bike. On his leather vest, I see the words "Heaven's Sinners". When he gets to his bike, he throws his leg over and yells, "Oh, and if I were you, I'd finish that pimp. He's one determined mother fucker."

Then he starts his bike, waves at his men, and disappears into the night. We all stand watching the empty road for a long moment, then Jackson turns to me.

"You got a lot of explainin' to do."

113

I open my mouth, but I quickly close it. I can't hide this away any longer. Not now I know for sure Jasper is going to great lengths to find me.

"It's a long story," I say, my voice full of defeat.

"Then best you start fuckin' talkin'," Jackson growls.

I nod and watch Jackson turn and walk towards his bike. When he gets on, he glares over at Cade.

"Go get on his bike, sugar. I'll follow."

I turn to face him. "What? Why?"

"Respect, that's why."

Understanding, I walk over to Jackson's bike. He thrusts a helmet angrily at me, and I put it on. Then I climb on the bike and wrap my arms around him. He's angry. I can feel his deep breathing. He starts his bike, and pulls onto the road. As we ride, the sound of the Harley's rumbling behind us, I consider how I'm going to tell them my story. They have an idea, but they don't know all of it. They don't even know the half of it. I have to tell them, which means I have to bare my soul to them. This is a moment I really was not looking forward to, but I can't back away now.

They aren't going to let me.

And part of me needs to be freed of this.

So I know it's time.

CHAPTER 13

PAST

"Mom?" I yell, watching my mother thrash on the ground.

There's froth coming from the corners of her mouth, a bloody, disgusting froth. Her eyes are rolling, her body is convulsing. She's having a reaction; she's taken too much. This time it's bad. I can tell it goes beyond all those other times. Her arms fly around as she struggles for air. My legs are glued to the floor, at least that's what it feels like. I want to go to her, but my body won't move. It's like I'm in a trance. All I can hear in my head are her words over the years. All I can recall are the painful, bitter memories of her.

"You'll be a whore too, Addison. You're destined to be the queen of scum."

"You're worthless. Just a bastard child and a thorn in my side."

"You'll never amount to anything. You'll never make anyone proud. You're nothing."

"Whore."

"Slut."

"Pathetic scum."

"Jasper is good for you. He'll teach you some manners."

I realize the tears are flowing when I blink and a rush of them tumble down my cheeks. My earliest memories, to my most recent ones, are that of the same. She never supported me; she never believed in me; she never helped me when Jasper put his dirty hands on me. When I was thirteen and bleeding from rape, she told me to toughen up. She never did the one simple thing all mothers should do for their kids – she never loved me.

As her body convulses, and she begins turning blue, I find myself unwilling to help her. I just stand, watching the last moments of her life, watching as it's all ripped from her.

When she takes her last gurgling breath, and her head flops to the side, my tears become heavier. That's also when the panic sets in. I just let my mother die. I just stood there and let her die. The next few minutes of my life, happen in a blur. Before I know it, I've packed a bag and I'm running down the street. I don't know where I'm going. I don't know if I'll ever come back. I'm just running. Before I get out of the alley beside my house, Jasper is there. He's always there. His face is frantic, and he has a phone in his hand. He's seen her; he knows what I did. When his eyes fall on me, he rushes over. I would continue to run, but my legs have turned to jelly.

"What the fuck have you done, snake!" he roars.

"She…she…she…took a drug overdose."

"You fuckin' little slut. This is your fault. It's all your fault. You were meant to be watchin' her. You were meant to be the one to keep this from happening. Instead, you run. She's my best girl. She owes me money. You'll pay for this."

As he steps towards me, I react how anyone in my position would. I lash out. I have to escape this life. I have to escape him. If I stay here, he'll turn me into her. He will make me the whore he made her. I'd rather die, but he won't let that happen either. Last time I tried, he had me at the hospital before the drugs even hit my system. He's keeping me alive because I'm his best asset and he knows it. So, the only way for me to be free, is to run. And the only way to run, is to get rid of him. I slide my fingers around to the back of my jeans where I tucked my mother's gun on the way out. I wasn't stepping out without protection. Not in a world as ugly as this. I point the gun at Jasper, and he stops, his face falling.

"Put that down!"

"You've made my life a living hell from the day you took my innocence without permission. You continued to rip every part of my soul to shreds, until there was nothing left."

"You do this, snake, and I'll make you pay," he growls, but his voice is shaky.

"There's nothing you could do, that you haven't already done."

"You're nothing," he growls. "Running won't make you anything. You hurt me, you're going to end up in jail, continuing to be a nothing. I allow you to survive."

"You allow me nothing!" I scream, my hands shaking.

"Without me, you're nothing! You run, you're dead. You shoot me, you're fucking dead!"

"I'll risk it."

I aim the gun down, and I press the trigger. I don't want to kill him. I don't have it in me. What I do have in me though, is the determination to make sure he never hurts another girl again, the way he did me. So, I shoot him in the crotch. Blood splatters over his legs and over the front of my shirt. My hands are trembling so hard the gun tumbles from my fingers. Jasper's mouth opens, and for a moment it remains like that, a silent scream. Then the piercing, high pitched roar escapes. He falls to the floor, and I take a few steps back. I stare at the gun on the floor, and his bleeding, convulsing form.

Before I run, I lean down and snatch up his phone. I open it and dial the police. The police are familiar with me; they have been for a long time. They were forever around helping my mother out when she didn't deserve it. When a familiar voice answers, it takes me a moment to get the words from my lips. My entire body feels numb. All I can feel is an odd prickling over my skin. Sweat trickles down my forehead and my legs are shaking so badly I struggle to stay upright. I let my own mother die, then I shot a man. Now, I don't

117

have a choice; I have to run but not before I finish this once and for all.

"Officer Kerry?" I whisper.

"Yes, who have I got?" his rough voice responds.

"It's…Addison."

"Addison, is everything okay?"

"My mother's dead. I found her this afternoon. Jasper was there. He turned on me, so I ran. He followed me and cornered me in an alley. I s-s-shot him in the crotch. I was afraid. He's alive, but there's lots of blood."

"Okay, Addison, it's going to be fine. You're not going to get into trouble for that. Sit tight. We're on our way. Are you sure your mother is gone?"

"Yes," I say. "Jasper killed her."

Then I hang up the phone, and I run.

For good this time.

~*PRESENT*~

As soon as we step into Jackson's house, he spins on us. His face is wild with rage. I know Cade dropping the 'my girl' bomb earlier didn't go down well.

"The fuck is goin' on?" he barks, crossing his arms.

"Addison and I…" Cade begins.

"Are fuckin' doin' nothing!" He spits. "Get your mother fuckin' hands off her. You're not fuckin' touchin' my daughter, Cade."

118

"Dad!" I yell, shocked that Jackson would try this one on.

"You started with a fucked up life," Jackson begins, giving me a look. "You ain't gonna finish with one."

"That's not your choice to make," I protest.

"He's no fuckin' good for you, Addison."

"Again," I say, keeping as calm as possible. "That's not your choice to make."

"Like fuck it ain't!"

"I'm twenty-one, Dad. Don't start trying to tell me what to do."

"Sugar, it's cool. Let him take his..." Cade begins.

"No," I snap, cutting him off. I look Jackson right in the eye. "You made a mistake once, you picked the wrong person and you got burned. I'm sorry for that, but you don't get to throw that on me. I want to be with Cade, and I want to be around you. If you won't let me have both, you know which one I'll choose."

Jackson glares at me. "That's blackmail, kid."

"You can't choose who I fall in love with, Dad."

Cade jerks a little beside me, but he says nothing.

"No, I fuckin' can't, but I can warn you that tangling yourself up in the biker life ain't the happily ever after you dreamed of."

"Who said happily ever after couldn't involve bikers?"

Jackson's lips twitch, and I know I've managed to soften him a bit. Taking the moment, I step forward. "I want to be in your life, but I want to be in Cade's, too. Don't make me choose. Please?"

"I just want the fuckin' best for you," he grumbles.

119

"Then let me choose, for the first time in my life, what I think is best for me."

Jackson sighs deeply, and then turns to Cade. "You fuckin' hurt her, so help me God, I'll fuckin' cut your dick off and feed it to you."

Cade nods. "I got ya, boss."

"You fuckin' treat her with respect. She ain't no whore, Cade."

I flinch now.

"No, she ain't," Cade says simply.

Jackson glares at Cade once more, I know he's still not happy with it, but he doesn't really have the grounds to fight it. He points to the table nearby.

"Sit, we all gotta talk."

We all take a seat, and I feel my chest begin to clench. I've been dreading this moment, and yet I so desperately want it off my chest.

"Start talkin', girl," Jackson says, giving me a soft look.

"I don't know where to start," I say in a small voice.

"From the beginning, sugar," Cade says.

I swallow, look down at my hands and begin telling them my story.

"When you mentioned Jasper's name a few weeks ago, Jackson, I wasn't honest. I said I knew of him. The truth is, he...he made my life a living hell. He was the one who took my virginity when I was thirteen."

Jackson is out of his chair before I can say another word. It skitters across the room and smashes into a nearby wall. He storms around, grips me from my chair by the shoulders and lifts me. He's powerful. I can feel it in the way he lifts me from the chair. He brings me close to his face. His eyes are wild. His body is trembling.

"All this time, all this fuckin' time you didn't tell me? How could you keep that from me? Fuckin' hell, Addison, why?"

My tears shock me because they're not something I want to show my father, let alone Cade.

"Because I didn't know you!" I scream.

He drops me, then I'm in his arms, and he's holding me tightly. I can feel his heart thudding against my cheek. His fingers tangle in my hair and he holds me close, and I sink into him. This comfort, is a comfort I have needed my entire life. God, Jackson, why weren't you around when I needed you?

"Baby," he rasps. "So fuckin' sorry. I should have fought harder for you."

I shake my head, soaking his jacket with my tears. "Why didn't you?" I croak.

"I tried, baby, I did. I looked for your Ma, but I couldn't find her. She gave me a false name. Then I searched for your name, couldn't find that either because apparently she changed your name as soon as she bolted. I figured maybe you were better off without me, and eventually, I stopped lookin'. Worst mistake I ever made."

I jerk, and he holds me tighter. When I finally pull back, he grips my face.

"Can't change what I did back then, but I can change what I do now. I'll find that fucker, and I'll make him pay for every moment he hurt you."

I nod, knowing he will do just that. I don't care either. Not one, tiny bit. I look past Jackson to see Cade sitting at the table, just staring at his hands. He's too still, too quiet. I step out of Jackson's grips, and gently walk over. I place my fingers on his arm and he flinches.

"Hey," I whisper.

He looks up at me, then he grinds out, "Keep goin' with the story, yeah?"

I stare at him a long moment before sitting back in my chair. I take a few deep breaths, wipe my face and continue once Jackson sits back down.

"So, after that, Jasper was a big part of my life. He was Mom's pimp; he was always around. He continued to rape me. Eventually, I stopped fighting him."

Jackson growls and Cade smashes the glass in his hand, splinters of it scatter across the table.

"Mother fuckin' little cunt will die, a slow, painful death," Cade barks.

"Cade, lock it up. Let her finish," Jackson rasps.

Cade's jaw ticks, but he nods for me to keep going. I rub my hands together, take a deep breath and keep going.

"He protected my mother in a sense; she was his best client. He supplied her with drugs, loads of them, but he held back her cash. If she did something wrong, he wouldn't pay her. Often we went for up to a week with such a small amount of food, a rat could barely survive. Drugs were the only way either of us could cope. I tried to avoid them as much as possible, and mostly I had the power. When Jasper came over though, it was the only way I could…get through. It was the only way I could deal. Anyway, this went on for years. The same shit, different days. Then Billy came along, he was my boyfriend. He caught Jasper one day, and he just about tore his…parts off. Jasper stayed away after that, but when Billy left, he came back. That day, I tried to kill myself. I took loads of ecstasy, but Jasper got me to the hospital before it did any damage. Things only got worse after that."

I stop to take a deep breath, and when I look up, both men are completely and utterly broken. I can see it in their faces. Cade is panting, his fists are clenched and there's blood dripping from his hand. Jackson's eyes are glassy and red, and he too, is panting.

"Cade, your hand is bleeding," I say.

"Keep. Talking."

His voice is firm, but gentle. I nod at him, and push a dish towel over the table. He grips it, and briefly his hand brushes mine. This gives me enough comfort to keep going.

"One day, I got home from the shop, and Mom was having a reaction to an overdose. She was frothing at the mouth, convulsing – I knew she'd taken too much and was going to die."

Tears begin streaming down my face as the guilt rips through my chest. I heave, and I feel Jackson's hand grip mine.

"I...I..." I choke out. "I stood there and watched her die. I didn't even call an ambulance until after she was dead. I let her life slip from her. I hated her so much, that I didn't even want to save her."

"Oh, baby," Jackson rasps.

"Sugar, it ain't your fault," Cade says in that gruff but gentle tone.

"It was my fault. I let her die. I should have saved her, but saving her meant I would continue to be trapped."

"You ain't to blame," Cade says again. "What happened after that?"

"I ran. I packed a bag, her gun and I ran. I was in the nearby alley when Jasper caught up to me. He made all kinds of threats, and I lost it. I shot him, right in the crotch. Then I called the police and I told them..."

"What sugar?" Cade encourages.

"I told them he killed her."

Both men stare at me in shock for a moment.

123

"That's why he's after you?" Jackson says.

"Yes, that and the fact that I blew his penis off."

"Fuckin' Christ, sugar, you should've told us," Cade growls.

"I didn't trust you. I didn't trust anyone. I was just going to run…"

"He would have found you," Jackson says. "Cade's right, you should've told us. We can protect you, Addison."

"I know that now," I say softly. "But I didn't then."

"Well, we have a fairly big problem on our hands now," Jackson says, standing. "We got an angry pimp who seems determined to get hold of you."

"What're you going to do?" I ask.

Jackson turns to me. "I'm going to track him down, then I'm going to blow his fuckin' brains out."

My entire body jerks.

"You'll go to jail," I say, hearing the panic in my voice.

"No, he won't, sugar. No one fucks with bikers."

I turn to Cade. "He's not a nice man."

Cade grins, stands and leans over the table. "Let me tell you somethin', sugar. Neither are we…"

I rub my fingers together, nervously. "What do we do now?"

Jackson gives me a determined look. "You stay at the compound during the day, at night, you're to have one of us with you at all times."

"Agreed," Cade nods.

Are they serious? Oh no, no freaking way. I've spent my life with chains on. I'm not going to do it again. Jasper doesn't scare me, and I will not be imprisoned while these guys overreact.

"No," I say, crossing my arms.

Both men turn to stare at me. "'Scuse me?" Cade says, his eyes flaring with anger.

"You heard me. I said, no. I'm not going to sit in this house, day in, day out, and spend all my spare time at the compound because of Jasper. He doesn't scare me and I won't live my life like that again. I ran away to be free, not to be held down again."

"Do you have any fuckin' idea how much time this pimp is putting into finding you?" Jackson hisses.

"I blew his dick off," I mutter. "Of course I know how much time he's putting into finding me."

"You ain't gettin' a say so in this, sugar," Cade says, his voice heavy with anger and frustration. "You will be doin' as you're told."

I slide my chair back, and walk towards the door. "You can't stop me. I can be careful. What I can't be is a prisoner."

"You fuckin' walk out that door, I'll make you wish you didn't," Cade warns.

"Whatever, biker," I snap.

"Addison, you best fuckin' do as he asks," Jackson growls.

I spin around glaring at both of them. "What are you going to do, tie me up?"

They both look at each other, and nod. Cade stands, stalking towards me. I throw my hands up.

"Cade, I swear to fucking God, if you try and stop me…"

He steps forward, leans down and lifts me, throwing me over his shoulder. I scream, pummeling my fists into his back.

"You asshole!"

"You think I'm fuckin' jokin' when it comes to your safety?" he growls, turns and walks towards the stairs. "Well, I'm fuckin' not. You're not goin' to walk out this door, sugar. End of fuckin' story."

"You can't do this!" I protest, pummeling my fists over and over on his back.

"Ah, yeah, sugar, I can and I am."

When he reaches the top of the stairs, he turns and begins heading toward my room.

"I can take care of myself," I growl.

"That's good to know, still ain't changin' my fuckin' mind."

"CADE!"

He walks into my room, and drops me on the bed.

"You fuckin' leave this house, sugar, and it won't be pretty."

"You…asshole!"

He grins at me. "Said that already babe. Now, get some sleep yeah?"

With a smirk, he turns and walks back towards the door. When he reaches it, he gives me one last glance.

"Oh and sugar? Try to escape, I'll put my hand on your ass."

Then he's gone. Fucking wanker.

I brood for a good hour, before deciding that I don't care what they said, I'm going to do what I want. Jasper doesn't frighten me, I've lived years with him. I walk over to the old window, and peer out of it. I can see that I could easily climb down. Quietly, though? I don't know. I slide the window up, and I can hear Cade and Jackson talking downstairs. My heart hammers as I climb out, gripping the large drain-pipe beside my window. I hope this sucker doesn't break. Using all the skills I learned over the years, when having to get out of tricky places, I latch on and begin slowly lowering myself down. It takes me a good fifteen minutes to get to the bottom, and by the time I get there, I'm shaking.

That will teach them to lock me away.

I lived long enough like that.

I sure as shit won't be doing it again.

~*CHAPTER 14*~

PRESENT

"Another beer," I yell at the bartender.

After much debate, I decide the bar is the best place to go. I'm not going to the compound, and I'm certainly not going to Cade's place. I figure the bar is a good choice. I need a break and I need to breathe, just for a moment. I know at this point Jasper doesn't know where I am. I'm safe for tonight. The bar I'm in is your typical biker bar. Most of the people in here are undesirable, but that's fine by me. I'm not here to start any fights. I'm just here to take a break. It's nice to be served for once, without having to do anything to earn it.

"Here ya go, girly," the old, burly bartender smiles.

"Thanks," I return the smile then spin around on my chair and watch the room.

Most people are sitting, making out, smoking, doing all the usual things. Some are playing pool on the old, well-worn pool table in the corner. A few are on the dance floor, wiggling and singing to the music. I lean back and sip my beer, and that's when I see them. I didn't notice them before, so they must have only just come in. It's Spike and a few of his club members. Most people are giving them a wide berth, and it doesn't surprise me considering how intimidating they look. They certainly aren't a group you would pick on. I take another swig of me beer, and watch as Spike lays his eyes on me. He grins, and it's wide and proud. He stands, sauntering through the crowd until he stops in front of me.

"Well, precious, you're the last person I thought I'd see here. Where's your bodyguard?"

I shrug, putting the beer down. The alcohol has hit my head now, and I am feeling relaxed and completely content.

"He doesn't own me."

Spike smirks. "Messin' with Cade ain't a wise idea."

I return his grin and stand. "Could say the same about myself."

I walk out onto the dance floor, and shove through the people until I find my own dancing spot. Then I begin dancing, throwing my hands in the air and wiggling my hips. Spike shoves through the crowd, stopping in front of me and tilting his head to the side.

"You ain't like anythin' I've ever seen. You had your life threatened today, and here you are dancin' like it don't matter," he says.

I smile at him. "I've had far worse than what you delivered to me tonight. I move on. I survive. This here, it's me surviving and doing what I have to do. Now, are you going to stand there staring at me, or are you going to dance with me?"

Spike grins, real big, then he reaches out and grips my hips. Girls nearby sigh as we begin to move. I know Cade will hate this. I know if he walked in right now, he would lose his shit. That's the point though, I'm trying to prove that no one owns me. Cade sparks things deep inside me, things that make me want to spend every waking minute with him, but that's just not enough for me to become the kind of girl that's ordered around and made into some pathetic little housewife that does as she's told. Yeah, that's never going to happen.

So, letting everything go, I dance, twirl, sing, and am having the time of my life. Spike continues to grin at me. He knows exactly what I'm doing and he knows the exact moment that Cade walks in too, because his face lights up. Whatever went down between these two, Spike is getting a complete thrill over the fact that I'm dancing with him. I see Cade from the corner of my eye, and the look on his face is beyond dangerous. I don't stop though. I just keep spinning around with Spike.

"I know exactly what you're doin', precious, but I'm goin' to step away now 'coz Cade's givin' you that look," Spike says to me, just after he's twirled me out and back in again.

"What look?" I ask, spinning and pressing my back to his chest.

"The look that says if I don't get my hands off you in three seconds, I'll be a bloody heap on the ground. So, I'm out," he says, letting me go. "Don't forget my money. I don't want to have to tell that sleaze ball where you are, but I will."

Then he disappears through the crowd. Before I can take another step, I feel firm hands wrap around my arms and spin me around. Cade is standing in front of me, looking so completely fuckable. He's gorgeous when he's mad. His green eyes almost go blue. His jaw clenches and his entire body becomes a stiff, rigid board.

"You dirty dance," he growls, leaning down to my ear. "It's with me."

I open my mouth to argue with him, but he slams his mouth down over mine so hard I taste blood. He slides a hand down my arm and then he curls it around my hip, pulling me close. He kisses me until I'm panting and my head is spinning. I'm wet for him, and God, aching to have him inside me. Something about his dominance makes me crave him.

"You kiss," he snarls. "It's with me."

He runs a finger down my belly, until he gets to the bottom of my skirt. He slides a finger up the inside of my thigh until he's stroking my damp panties.

"You get fuckin' touched, it's by me."

His voice is raspy, but mostly it's dangerous.

"You fuck," he hisses. "It's with my fuckin' cock inside you."

I open my mouth again, but he cuts me off with a sharp look that dares me to keep playing this game with him.

130

"And sugar," he murmurs, leaning close, "if you ever play with me like that again, you won't like how it ends. That ain't a fuckin' threat either; it's a mother fuckin' promise."

Then he spins, taking me with him as he shoves through the crowd. Sweet mother of God, why do his words make me want him so much more?

~*~*~*~

I don't know what I expected Cade to do, but what he does, has my head spinning. He takes me to a private bar out the back, and locks the door. It's empty, and my guess, not used a great deal. I watch as he stalks over to the bar and walks around, picking up a bottle of whiskey. He flicks the top off, and puts it to his mouth, drinking. I watch as his throat moves, and oh my, I think my panties just went from soaked to drenched. When he puts the bottle down, he opens the nearby freezer and pulls out some ice. He shrugs off his leather jacket, grips the hem of his shirt and tears it off. I stare, eyes wide.

Cade is fucking beautiful. Every inch of him would make any woman's panties soaked in seconds. He comes around the bar and stops in front of me. His face is hard to read, but I can still see the lingering anger behind his stony expression. He's angry at me. No, he's fucking wild at me. Understandable, I suppose. I watch as he reaches down, gripping his jeans and popping the top button. I swallow and my palms become damp. When he lowers them and his cock springs free, I can't help licking my lips. He steps forward, gripping my jaw and running his thumb over my bottom lip. His gaze is intense, fierce, even a touch feral. He grips a couple of ice cubes, and puts them towards my mouth.

"Suck these, then get on your knees, and suck my cock, sugar."

Well shit. When he says it like that, so demanding, so powerful, I'm unable to do anything put part my lips and let him slip an ice cube into my mouth. I use my tongue to push the cubes around, letting them cool my mouth. When they've dissolved, I begin lowering to my knees. Cade's cock is in front of me, hard, throbbing, so fucking beautiful. I am desperate to taste him again, to slide him deep inside my throat, to feel his cum spurting and his cock pulsing as he shares his pleasure with me.

"Suck me, baby, hard."

Hard. Oh God. I grip his cock with my hand, gently sliding my palm up and down the hard length. He growls and tangles his fingers in my hair, and then he pulls my head forward, pressing his head into my parted lips. He hisses when I close my cold mouth around him. I've heard the ice cube trick is quite pleasurable for a man, but it's not something I've ever experienced. Cade grunts and thrusts his hips, sliding his entire length into my mouth. I open further to accommodate his massive size and then I curl my lips around my teeth and let him fuck my mouth any way he pleases. I feel him slip an ice cube into the side of my mouth, and his groans as it begins to melt are out of this world.

"Mouth so fuckin' sweet," he growls. "So fuckin' sweet."

I gasp and reach up, gripping his backside and clenching my nails into his skin as he continues to thrust, harder, faster, until he's quite literally fucking my face. He's pounding into my mouth, his cock stretching my lips, causing them to burn in the most pleasurable way. I reach down, slipping my finger up under my skirt to find my clit. Cade tugs my hair, causing me to wince.

"Get your fuckin' fingers outta that cunt, it's mine."

Whimpering, I remove my fingers. Cade pulls his cock from my now swollen, cold lips and stares down at me.

"I'm not wastin' that in your mouth. I'm goin' to fuck you on that bar and you're goin' to be full of ice. I'm also goin' to put my hand on your ass, so get ready."

I find myself nodding, even though I'm sure this isn't how I had planned the night to end. Cade leans down, pulling me to my feet. He slides his lips over mine, and the feeling of his warm, heated lips dancing with my cold, swollen lips is purely erotic. I grip his chest, squeezing and feeling the muscles bunching underneath my palms. God, he's fucking yummy. I want more of him. I want so much that I can't breathe. I need it until it's all I can think about, all I can dream about.

"Lay down on the bar, sugar," Cade orders.

I do as he asks, walking over and sliding my bottom up onto the bar. I lay my back down on the old, faded timber and prop my legs on a nearby stool. Cade growls, and walks over, wearing only his jeans, which are now half way down his ass. His cock still stands proudly, aching for more. Cade grips my panties and slides them down my legs. Then he grips my ankles and places my legs even further apart. He growls with satisfaction, and then he takes hold of a couple of ice cubes, gently pressing them to my entrance. I squirm as he slips one inside me, his finger sliding in deep, filling me, stretching me. I groan at the strange, cool sensation and buck my hips, wanting more.

"Patience, sugar."

He grips another cube, sliding it in behind the first one. I cry out as they fill and stretch me, and his fingers stir my sensitive spots until I'm crying out and begging him to let me come. He keeps his finger inside me, and with his other hand, he takes a cube and rubs it over my clit, while he thrusts his finger in and out. The feeling of the freezing cube on my throbbing clit is out of this world. My back arches, and electric bolts of pleasure jerk my body. I reach up, gripping my own hair as the pleasure becomes too intense. It's so different, so fucking incredible. When I come, I come hard. I scream out Cade's name and my body thrashes on the old bar.

"Fuckin' beautiful," Cade husks as he slips his fingers from my body. "Don't move, sugar, I'm goin' to fuck you hard."

133

I squirm at his words, but I stay on the bar. I hear Cade shuffling around, and I can feel the cool ice cubes beginning to melt inside me, sliding down my ass and causing me to shiver. I hear the sound of a small stool scraping across the floor, and then Cade is over me, his body looming over mine. He wraps his fingers in my hair and leans down close.

"You clean, sugar?"

"What?" I whisper.

"Clean, have you been checked?"

I flush. "No, I haven't."

He tilts his head to the side. "You're goin' to get checked, yeah? For now, we'll use a condom."

For now. Sweet heaven. Cade leans back off me, and I lift my head to watch as he rolls a condom over his hard length. Then he's standing straight, gripping my hips and sliding me to the end of the bar. When my ass is just about hanging over the edge, he tilts my hips up and drives into me, with one hard thrust. I cry out, bucking as the feeling of him pushing the ice cubes deep inside me sends shivers up my spine. Holy shit. Holy fucking shit. He pulls his entire length out with a feral hiss, then he drives it back in. I whimper, arching and sliding my fingers up my top to grip my breasts.

"Yeah, fuckin' touch them for me, baby," Cade growls.

I shove my shirt up and cup my breasts, rolling my nipples in my fingers. Cade groans so deeply, and so fucking primal it causes me to clench hard around him.

"Fuck, sugar, squeeze my dick again."

I love when he talks dirty.

"Talk dirty to me," I beg, clenching around him again.

"Your little cunt is so tight around me. Fuck, sugar, I wanna come so fuckin' hard."

"Then come," I rasp, feeling my own release rising higher and higher as Cade thrusts harder and harder.

"Not 'till you," he grates out, his jaw tense, his eyes closed.

I squeeze my nipples harder, and when Cade thrusts deep once more, I come. I come so hard my entire world spins. I don't even scream, because I've gone beyond that. All that escapes my mouth is a pathetic strangled sound. Cade does as promised, and brings his hand down hard over my thigh as he throws his head back and I feel his cock begin to pulse as he comes with me. Together, we ride our high until we've both stopped shaking. Cade leans down, grips my shoulders and pulls me up. He presses my cheek to his chest, and I slide my tongue out, licking the fine layer of salty sweat from his skin. He shudders and holds me tighter.

"Fuck, sugar, you're sendin' me over the edge, and I'm lovin' every second of it."

If I was being honest with myself, I'd say I felt exactly the same.

"I shouldn't have run out earlier," I murmur against his skin.

He pulls back and looks down at me with a hard expression.

"Took every strength in me tonight, not to make a scene in that bar. The only fuckin' reason I didn't, is 'coz it's what Spike wants. Sugar, if you ever fuckin' think that I won't tie you up if you're bein' like that, you're wrong. I will. I'll do whatever it fuckin' takes to protect you, don't fuckin' put it past me."

I swallow. God, why is it that the idea of him doing that both thrills and frightens me?

"I get it," I whisper, meeting his hard gaze.

"I won't be fucked with. You don't ever do that to me again. Do you feel me?"

I nod. "I feel you."

"You're mine. You can argue that, you can run, you can play games, but the in the end, the result is still the same. I won't be lettin' you go anytime soon. Best you fuckin' learn to live with it. If I didn't think you wanted this as much as me, I would let you walk away, but you know as well as I do, this goes far deeper than sex."

He's right about that, and I know it. "I hear you," I whisper, dropping my lips to the spot between his nipples and licking.

"Stop lickin' me, baby. It's makin' my dick hard again and we don't have time to fuck anymore."

I stare up at him and pout. He grins, flicking my lower lip. "Don't worry, baby, we're goin' to fuck again. It just ain't gonna be here."

"Why not? It was fun."

He smirks and then nods towards the door. I spin around to see Spike standing, watching us through a small window. I gasp and press my hands over my chest.

"What the fuck, Spike!" I shriek.

"Spike, fuck off," Cade says in a warning tone.

Spike grins, and then turns and disappears. I spin to Cade, my mouth open in shock.

"What the hell? Did you know he was there?"

"Fuck no, sugar. Not until a minute ago. Didn't surprise me though."

"What? Is he some sort of sicko?"

Cade grins. "Spike has certain fetishes. He's got one hell of a sex drive. He don't mind watchin' here and there."

136

"And that doesn't bother you?" I huff, moving away from him and finding my skirt.

"It would if he was there the whole time, but he wasn't. He caught the last minute, if that."

"Sick bastard," I snap, dragging my skirt up my hips.

"We all got our fantasies, sugar. Spike likes the act of sex, and he likes watching it. He also has other fetishes that really don't need to be discussed."

"I'll never look at him the same again."

Cade chuckles and pulls on his shirt. "You get used to it."

"Has he watched you before?"

Cade shrugs. "He's watched a few times when I've fucked a girl. Mostly though, he fucked her with me."

My mouth drops open and I stop mid-way through pulling my shirt down. "What?" I gasp.

He shakes his head and puts a heavily ringed hand up. "Was in the past, sugar. Didn't do much for me. It was only a few times."

"You...you...like threesomes?"

He walks over, gripping my shoulders. "I had a few. They weren't all they were cracked up to be. Haven't had one in a solid five or six years. Don't stress your pretty little head about it."

I nod. I guess I can understand the fascination. Hell, it was me who stood watching Cade and Britney only a month ago. I adjust my clothes, and watch as Cade dresses himself.

"Hey, Cade?"

"Yeah, baby?"

"Spike…"

"Not now, sugar, I'll tell you tonight. We gotta swing by the compound first."

I guess I'll leave that one alone.

For now, anyway.

~*CHAPTER 15*~

PRESENT

The compound is full when we arrive. As soon as we walk inside, Jackson is up and storming over. Cade puts his hand up, stopping him.

"I got it. We're all good. She won't run off again. Will you, sugar?"

The tone of his voice tells me I wouldn't dare try that one again.

"No," I whisper. "I won't."

"You have no fuckin' idea how much you scared me," Jackson growls.

"Sorry, Dad."

His face drops. Just like that his expression changes from that of anger, to that of pure agony. My words hit him hard, but they hit him in the best possible way. I know how much it means to him, and in a way, it means a lot to me too. I care about Jackson, and I want to grow to love him and be in his life. Perhaps this is how my story is meant to be told. I could run, but I'd be alone. Here, I have people who want to take care of me. Were they what I would have picked for myself? No. Sometimes though, it's the things you least expect that are the most beautiful.

"Aw fuck kid, you're killin' me."

I smile, and he returns it. Warmly. Jackson and I are growing closer and closer by the minute, and I'm loving it.

"Knew one day I'd get you back. This time though, you're not goin' again."

I step back to Cade's side and wrap my arm around his mid-section. "I don't plan to."

Jackson nods, and he still doesn't look happy about Cade and I. I have no doubt that if Jackson had been involved in my life from an earlier age, that he wouldn't have given in so easily. He wasn't in my life though, and I know he's not willing to risk losing me again. I'm glad he didn't cause too much of a scene. I don't want to lose either of them.

"Well, guess you two should sit down and join this discussion," he says.

Cade and I join the other bikers, and I nod at each of them. They all return the nods, giving me and Cade curious expressions.

"You boys ought to know, Addi is now my Old Lady. You know what that means; you treat her with the upmost fuckin' respect, and if you don't, I'll fuck you up."

I give Cade a glare; he knows that I hate the Old Lady thing. It sounds so…well…old. Cade grins at me, utterly proud of his efforts. Rolling my eyes, I turn back to the group and listen as Jackson starts talking, but only after giving Cade a glare.

"As you know, women do not attend these meetings. Addi, as Cade's Old Lady, you will have to learn the rules around here. Number one rule, you don't come on rides unless those rides are for Charity's or similar. You don't join in on our weekly church meetings and you don't get a say so in what we involve ourselves in. As my daughter, you're automatically under our protection, but considering you're also Cade's old lady, that protection increases. You don't enter the back sheds, those are women free – no argument. The only reason you're here tonight, is 'coz we need your information to track this mongrel down. Got me?"

Well damn, maybe I should ask permission to piss too! I want to give them a smart retort, but I know this is important to them, and if I want their respect, I have to earn it.

"I understand," I say.

Cade squeezes my hand. "Atta girl, sugar."

"Don't think I'm slaving over a hot stove for you, biker."

He chuckles and the rest of the guys laugh. "Got ya," he grins.

"All right, now that's outta the way, let's get to the issue of that pimp," Jackson announces.

"We got any idea where to find him?" Cade asks.

"No," Jackson says, then he turns to me. "But I imagine you know, Addi?"

The idea of going back…there…it bothers me. I jerk and Cade squeezes my hand harder.

"We ain't gonna let him touch you, sugar. You tell us what you know."

I sigh deeply, and then I answer Jackson. "I know where he runs his show, yeah."

"You give us an address, and we'll pay him a visit."

I rattle off Jasper's address and Jackson writes it down.

"He may not be there," I say. "After what happened, it's likely he moved."

"It's a start, baby," Cade says, before he turns to Jackson. "When do we ride?"

"First light."

"You're going tomorrow?" I say, shocked.

"Sooner he's gone, the better."

"Have you thought about asking Spike?" I suggest.

"Asked him. Spike don't know where Jasper is. He was contacted through Jasper's sources."

I let out a puff of air and run my fingers through my messy hair. "Well, I can only hope Jasper is where I left him."

"Yeah, can only hope so," Jackson says, then he faces the group. "Next issue, Spike."

"Spike's an issue? I thought he was backing down?" I blurt.

Jackson raises his brows at me, and I quickly shut my mouth and sink back into the chair.

"Spike's back in town, and I am pretty sure Ciara doesn't know."

Who the hell is Ciara? Cade notices my confused expression and mouths 'I'll tell you later.'

"She don't know. I spoke to her earlier," Bingo, a younger biker, says.

"We both know Spike and Ciara don't see eye to eye. If he's in town to bother her, we need to make sure his plans change," Jackson says, his voice deadpan.

"We'll get onto it, make sure she's kept outta his way," Bingo says.

"Good man, well, that's about all we have that Addi can hear," Jackson says, giving me a look.

I stand, putting my hands up. "Got it. I'll go and check on the bar."

"I'll be behind you soon, sugar," Cade says.

I nod and then I turn and leave the room, still curious as to who this Ciara chick is. There's a link somewhere, between Spike, Cade and clearly this girl. Was she someone they both…ummm…tag teamed? Did Cade steal Spike's girl? Or the other way around? They seem quite determined to keep her and Spike apart, so there's clearly some history there. I just don't know what. I get to the bar without noticing how much ground I've covered. I'm far too curious about this mystery girl. When I get in, Mindy is serving, and flirting. Girl can't keep those legs closed. I go to step towards her, when Britney steps in front of me. Rolling my eyes, I take a step back.

"Britney, I thought we covered that you and I don't get along and I don't play nice with the other kids," I say sarcastically.

"You don't scare me," she growls, jutting her perky breasts out.

"I wasn't trying to scare you. God, will you put those away, they're frightening the bikers."

I hear a group of bikers behind me roar with laughter. Britney's cheeks flush red and she leans in close.

"You're pushing it with me. I will make you pay, Addison. I don't care if you're Cade's Old Lady or if you're Jackson's daughter. You and I will have our day. I know what went down tonight, everyone knows. Well, you're the only one that doesn't know about Spike and Cade. I wonder why he hasn't told you yet? Perhaps he doesn't trust you. He told me right away."

This hurts my heart, but I don't let it show.

"What makes you think I don't know?" I say in a bored tone, while picking my nails.

"I know you don't, because you wouldn't be standing here if you knew what he did. Spike is the innocent one here."

Innocent? What is she talking about? Cade speaks of guilt, Britney speaks of innocence. Where is the connection?

143

"Maybe I have a heart and don't judge. Perhaps you should try it."

I step past her, but she grips my arm, digging her nails into my skin.

"Britney," Cade's voice booms across the room, "get your fuckin' hands of my woman."

Britney flinches and drops my arm. She leans in close and whispers, "This isn't over." Then she disappears before Cade reaches me.

"What the fuck was that about?" Cade demands as soon as he stops.

"Why don't you tell me?"

He puts his hands up and indicates that I should let him know what the hell I'm on about.

"Don't pretend you don't know. You told her things you clearly don't want to tell me. You and Spike…she knows right?"

Cade makes a growling sound and leans close. "Get your shit, and get out to my bike."

"Stop ordering me around!" I snap, crossing my arms.

"Sugar, what the fuck did I say about games? I don't fuckin' play them. You ain't gonna make a scene about somethin' you don't know. Get out to my bike, shut your mouth and we'll talk."

"I hate you when you're bossy," I say, before spinning on my heel.

"You fuckin' love me, you moody little shit."

I am smiling by the time I get out to his bike. He steps up behind me just as I'm reaching for my helmet, and he wraps his arms around my waist, pressing his lips to my neck.

"Love it when you're so fuckin' temperamental."

I grin and turn my head, pressing my lips to his. He spins me around, pressing my bottom against the bike seat, putting himself between my legs. He kisses me with intensity, sweeping his tongue across mine and every now and then, and stopping to nibble on my lower lip. I shudder and press myself against him. His hands wrap around me, and he pulls me as close as I can possibly get. He lets my lips go, and kisses up and down my cheeks until he finds my neck. He nibbles and sucks until I'm panting and desperate for him once more. Damn him for having such a powerful effect on me.

"You going to tell me about Spike?" I murmur against his cheek.

"Yeah, baby."

I let him set me back and slip my helmet on, and then I climb onto the bike behind him. He speeds out onto the road, and when we go right past his house, I'm confused. Until we pull up at Jackson's house. A little more of my heart opens up for him in that moment, because out of respect to my dad, he's taken me home instead of taking me to his house. We climb off the bike, and as soon as he's taken his helmet off, I grip him and kiss him deeply.

He pulls back after some sweet as hell dips of his tongue into my mouth, and murmurs, "What was that for?"

"For being so damn sweet."

He grunts. "Fuckin' sweet, think you got me all wrong, sugar."

I grin. "No, I think I got you all right, biker."

Another grunt. "Take me to your room, we gotta talk."

I do just that. I take his hand, and walk into my new home with a whole new outlook.

My life is finally piecing itself together.

And I couldn't be happier about it.

~*CHAPTER 16*~

PRESENT

"It's not a pretty story," Cade says when we're finally curled in the bed together.

"Mine wasn't pretty either," I remind him.

"Sugar, mine's a whole lot worse."

"Tell me. I won't judge you."

"Don't be so sure about that."

I don't say anything, I just lay quietly. I know he'll start talking when he's ready to. He begins speaking in a rough, scratchy tone and I can hear the emotion in his voice. I know why too, because when he tells me his story, it quite literally rips my heart out, stomps on it, and then rolls over it until there's nothing left but a battered mess. His story, is without a doubt, one of the most gut-wrenching stories I've ever heard. It makes my heart ache for him, but not just for him, for Spike too.

~*PAST*~

CADE

"We don't have a choice," Spike says, pacing the room.

"You can't fuckin' leave her in the house, Spike. It ain't safe."

He turns, glaring at me. "What the fuck should I do then?"

"Get her outta town. Throw her in the car and get her outta town."

"They're fuckin' everywhere. How the fuck do you think we can get her out?" Spike roars, driving his fist into a nearby table.

"We don't have a choice. You leave her here, her life is at risk."

"Fuck, Cade, fuck."

I walk over, grip his shoulder and jerk him to face me. Spike and I have been friends since we were kids. I know him. I trust him, and right now, he's in a fuck of a situation. He's got the biggest biker gang in the state after him, because of a dodgy drug job he did. Then the fucker tried to run, and made it a whole lot worse. Now, he's in deep shit, and so is his family. This gang, they don't give a fuck; they will put a bullet in his wife to prove a point. They're vulgar, rotten and downright deadly.

"Get Cheyenne and get her in the car. We'll drive her out of state, then we'll come back and deal with Hogan and his gang."

Spike runs his fingers through his hair, he's clearly distressed. He's gotten not only himself, but Chey in a situation that's beyond dangerous.

"I don't know if tryin' to get out is the best move, Cade."

"What will you do then? Leave her here? They come lookin' for you, they're goin' to come here. You need to get her out."

"I'll lock her in the basement; she'll be safe. I'll go face them, keep them away from the house."

"That's a fuckin' risk and you know it."

He growls. "Fuck, mother fucker."

"Go and get her. We're gettin' her out now."

"What's going on?"

We both turn to see Chey standing at the door. She's a beautiful woman, with silky blonde hair, big brown eyes and a tiny petite build. Her stomach is just starting to round out with their unborn babe. Chey is the love of Spike's life; he's given up everything to make her happy, to be with her, to adore her. And he does, he adores the living shit out of her. I watch as he walks over, wrapping his arms around her. Compared to his height, she looks like a child. Her head rests on his chest; he's a good foot taller than her. He holds her close, and for a moment, I let him. Time is running short though, Hogan's gang is already in town. It won't take them long to find Spike's address.

"We gotta move, Spike."

Spike let's Chey go and looks down at her. "We're goin' to have to go for a drive, sunshine? Got me?"

She nods. "What's going on?"

"Just a biker problem, Cade here is goin' to sort it for us, okay?"

She looks at me, her eyes hopeful. I smile at her, giving her the best reassuring glance I can. "Just goin' for a few days, yeah?"

She nods, and turns and quickly gathers her purse. "I can get clothes on the way."

Spike meets my gaze and I nod at him, then I grip the keys and jerk my head towards the garage. "My car."

"Haven't you two been drinking?" Chey asks.

"It'll be fine," I assure her.

"I have an unborn child. I'm not comfortable with you two driving."

Fuckin' women, they can be so fuckin' stubborn.

"Let Cade drive," Spike says in a warning tone.

"No," Chey says, crossing her arms.

"Might be a good idea to let her drive," I suggest. "If they see her, and we're low in the back seat, they won't get suspicious."

"Great idea, can we go?" Chey says, grabbing the keys out of my hand.

I can see she's scared as hell, but she's covering it well.

"I say no," Spike argues. "It's not safe."

"Spike, just let it be. It's the safest option."

"For who?" he roars at me. "You and me?"

"They won't recognize her!"

"You underestimate them!" Spike bellows.

Chey walks over, rubbing Spike's shoulder. "Hey, it's okay. I'm with Cade on this one; he's got the right idea. It'll be fine, honey, just fine."

Spike is trembling with rage, but he nods with defeat and we all pile into the car. Spike and I get into the backseat, and Chey gets into the front.

"Stay low, boys. I'll tell you when it's clear."

We both sit low as Chey backs out. When she's out on the road, I can feel Spike trembling beside me. He's scared, and I know why. These guys aren't the sort you fuck with. Jack's and the boys are out of town, so I can't even call on them for backup. This is our only option, and it's a shitty one.

"It's clear so far," Chey says from the front seat.

"Keep drivin' sunshine, yeah, good girl," Spike encourages, his voice trembling.

We drive for ten minutes and thus far, things are workin' out. Then everything changes. Just like that, it all becomes a nightmare.

"Spike, there's some bikes behind me," Chey says in a panicked voice.

"Fuck," Spike growls lifting his head enough to look out the back of the car.

"Is it them?" I ask, reaching into my jeans for my gun.

"Fuckin' mother fucker. It's them all right, with back up. There's at least twenty of them."

Fuck.

"Keep drivin', Chey," I say gently to the woman having a panic attack in the front of the car.

"Spike, I'm frightened," she wails.

"Baby, you're gonna be just fine," Spike soothes her, but his eyes are wide and panicked.

"Oh God, I don't want to get hurt. I don't want to," she sobs.

"Hey, Chey, listen to me, yeah? You're gonna be just fine. It's fine. You just keep drivin', sugar, just keep drivin'," I say to her, using my best comforting voice; even though right now, I'm anything but comforted.

"I say pull over," Spike growls in my ear. "Let me face them. It's me they want."

"They'll fuckin' kill you," I hiss.

"I'm not riskin' her."

"I won't pull over!" Chey cries, picking up speed.

"Chey, baby, do as I ask," Spike orders.

151

"No, I won't hand you to them," she cries, high pitched and frightened. "I won't let you die."

"We gotta pull over, Chey, pull over," Spike pushes.

"No!"

"Spike, she's right. We can't pull over," I hiss in his ear. "They'll blow your fuckin' brains out as soon as you step outta this car."

"Oh God!" Chey cries.

"It's me or they're goin' to fuckin' blow this car!"

"We're on a highway. They won't do anythin' while we remain on it."

"Cade, you're fuckin' wrong about this. It's the wrong call. We need to pull over."

"I won't fuckin' sit back and let my best friend die," I roar at him.

"Stop it!" Chey screams. "Just stop! I won't pull over!"

"Pull over!" Spike bellows. "Now, Cheyenne!"

"No!"

My heart is thudding so loudly I can hear it in my head. We're fucked. We're royally fucked. Spike grips the door handle, but I lunge at him, gripping him around the neck and hurling him backwards. That's when the shot rings out. Just one single shot. For a moment, I think it was just a warning shot, until I realize we're covered in blood. It's everywhere, on the roof, on the seats, on us. Spike's eyes are wide; he's just stopped moving. The whites in his eyes keep getting bigger and bigger, like he's in shock. My stomach drops. My buddy, they've shot him, fuck, no. Then he opens his mouth, and he screams. He screams so loudly my ears begin ringing. It's only then, I realize what he's screaming about.

It wasn't Spike who was shot.

It was Cheyenne.

Slowly, my mind registers what's happening. When my eyes fall on the front seat of the car, I see so much blood it's hard to see anything else. Then I see her, Cheyenne, missing half of her head. They shot her, clean in the back of the head. She's dead. It's her blood covering us. Spike's screams pierce my ears, and I can't react, all I can do is stare as the car begins spinning wildly out of control. When it begins to roll, I finally give in to the shock ripping through my body. Cheyenne is dead. She's dead and it's my fault. I let my best friend's wife die. I as good as killed her.

When the car smashes into a tree, I let everything go black.

It's easier that way.

~*PRESENT*~

I'm crying. No, I'm heaving. When Cade has finished telling me his story, I can hardly breathe. I've never heard something so gut wrenching in my life. It all makes sense to me now. God, poor Cade, poor Spike, poor Cheyenne. My heart breaks a little for each of them. I swipe my tears from my eyes, and I try to focus on Cade. He's staring out the window, his body heaving. The guilt he's holding, it's huge. He blames himself for Chey's death. I can understand why he blames himself, but he was trying to do the right thing. It's not on him, though I understand why he can't see that.

"I'm so sorry," I whisper, reaching out and placing my hand on his back.

He's sitting now, he got up mid-way through telling his story. He flinches when my fingers slide down his back.

"I killed my best friend's wife," he says in a voice devoid of all emotion.

"No, you didn't."

He turns, and when his eyes fall on mine, they're glassy and red. "Yeah, I fuckin' did. I forced them into that car. I didn't let him stop when he wanted to."

"If you didn't leave, it could have ended the same way. If you had let Spike out, do you think you wouldn't be carrying the same guilt when they did the same to him?"

Cade closes his eyes a moment, then opens them. "He hates me for it, and he has every fuckin' right."

"He can hate you, and yeah, maybe he does have the right, but he should hate himself too. He put himself in that situation, therefore putting his wife in it, too."

"He went through hell afterwards. Her family tried to put him in jail. He also lost a baby when she died. He lost everything he believed in."

"And he lost you."

Cade flinches. "I'll never forgive myself for it. I see her face every time I close my eyes. She haunts me."

"She wouldn't hate you, you know."

He shakes his head. "No, that's the fuckin' painful thing. She wouldn't hate me. She would tell me it was her choice. That she was the one who wanted it. Cheyenne was beautiful like that."

"I don't think you're a bad person, Cade."

He turns to look at me. "Why do you have to be so fuckin' understandin'?"

"Because I've lived with pain, guilt and horror before. I know how it feels to be trapped in it. You're not a bad person. You're only human, and sometimes, we don't make the right choices."

154

He cups my face. "I could so easily love you sugar, you're testin' every part of me. I'm fallin' fuckin' hard."

I tremble at his words and every hair on my body stands on end. Did he just say he could love me? I mean, truly love me? He must be mistaken. He's feeling lust, and getting it confused with falling in love. Noticing my expression, Cade turns my face and lets his eyes scan my face.

"Sugar, you look like you're about to pass out. Breathe."

I swallow over and over, unable to push the words from my head. He could love me. This can't be right, surely there's a mistake.

"You reactin' like this 'coz I said I'm fallin' in love with you, yeah?"

I nod, feeling my eyes sting.

"Ain't never had someone say that, and truly mean it, have you?"

I shake my head, and struggle to get a breath in.

"Well, I mean it, sugar, with everything I am. I don't love easily, and I sure as shit don't tell people when it's happenin'. You're different You've been different since the moment you walked into that compound."

"That's so cliché," I say, then burst out into a fit of nervous giggles.

Cade chuckles, and leans down, kissing my lips softly. "Cliché I can do for you, sugar."

"Now that's love," I whisper.

His green eyes scan my face, and then he leans forward and presses his lips to mine. We kiss softly for a long moment, just comforting each other in the only way we know how.

"Who is Ciara?" I ask when we finally pull apart.

"Ciara is Cheyenne's sister."

155

Oh. My. God.

"Why is she basically under the protection of the bikers?"

"Her and Spike don't exactly see eye to eye. They have had more run ins then I can begin to count. She blamed him."

"She doesn't blame you?" I whisper.

"No. She thinks if Spike never married Chey, like they all wanted, then it wouldn't have happened. He was warned away from her; he didn't listen. Back then, Spike lived a far more dangerous life then he lives now. He was muddled up in some fucked up shit, and that's how it ended for him."

"And now Ciara hates him?"

"Ciara blamed him, but she doesn't hate him. From what I know, Ciara had a massive crush on Spike before Chey came into the picture. Part of their issue goes back to that. The reason we protect her, is because when they start on each other, it's hard to stop it."

"Sounds complicated," I murmur.

"It's beyond complicated, sugar."

I lay down on my pillow with a deep yawn. I'm exhausted and emotionally drained. Cade gives me a small grin, and leans down, brushing his lips across my head. "Get some sleep, yeah? I'll be downstairs."

"What?" I say, rubbing my eyes to stop them from closing.

"I'm not leavin' you in a house alone when that crazy fucker is out there."

"You can't just sit downstairs and wait."

He gives me a look. "Can't I?"

"Cade…"

156

"Sugar..."

"Jackson will be home soon, I won't sleep if you're sitting down there alone."

"Then I'll sit here and watch you."

"That's creepy," I grumble.

"Sugar, I'm fuckin' stayin'. Now shut the fuck up, and get some sleep."

I narrow my eyes at him. "You know, you could say it nicely."

"Nah, sugar. Only way that works with you is when I tell it how it is. Now close your eyes and sleep."

"Yes, boss."

He gives me a stern look, so with a sigh I close my eyes. I'm out before either of us can get another word in.

I guess I was exhausted.

~*PRESENT*~

There's so much blood. It's everywhere. I'm screaming, but no one can hear me. Why won't anyone help me? I'm trapped. There's so much blood I can't find my way out. It's everywhere. On the walls, on the floor, and the roof. God, I can't escape it. I crawl, trying desperately to find a way out of this hell. I can hear screaming, high pitched, frightened. It's filling my mind, burning into me. I shake my head from side to side. Please stop, just stop so I can get out.

"Snake, there you are."

Jasper is suddenly in front of me, and at his feet is a dead woman. I scream at the sight of the gaping hole in her head. I can still hear screaming. It's a man.

157

"Cheyenne!" the voice cries, and I realize it's Spike.

The woman on the floor is Cheyenne, and the blood is hers. Jasper steps closer to me as I try to crawl away.

"I'll find you, snake, and this will be you."

God, help me, someone help me.

"Please, let me go!" I cry.

I bump into something, and I look down to see another dead body. It's Cheyenne again. How did she get here? I scream, but no sound comes out. Suddenly, her face is my mother's. Her skin is blue. She's struggling to breathe. I scream, this time it's ear splitting.

"Cheyenne," Spike screams again.

"Snake, you're mine," Jasper growls. "I'll kill you."

I bolt upright, screaming. My hands frantically grab at the sheets. I can't breathe. It hurts to even try. The door swings open, and Jackson comes running in, shirtless, sleep ruffled and waving a gun around.

"The fuck?" he roars.

I'm panting and sweating. The dream, it was awful. I wrap my arms around myself and I begin to cry. Jackson lowers the gun when he realizes there's no one in the room.

"Addi?" he says gently.

"It was just a dream," I croak through my tears.

"Ah shit," he murmurs, walking over to the side of the bed and wrapping his arms around me. I fall into him, and I begin to cry harder.

"Cade told me about Cheyenne tonight, and it just brought up so much for me. I killed her, Dad. I let her die right in front of me. I didn't call an ambulance. I didn't stick my fingers down her throat to make her sick it all up. I just let her die."

"She fucked you up. When someone fucks you up that bad, you don't wanna save them. What you did, anyone would have done."

"She was my mother," I wail.

"She gave birth to you. Didn't make her your fuckin' mother – it takes far more than that to be a mother."

"I let her die."

"You set her free."

I flinch, his words hitting me to my very core.

"Do you think that's the life she dreamed of having?" he says gently. "It's not. The short while I knew your ma, told me that she never wanted any of that. When you're so wrapped up in something like that, you can't escape it. She had no way out. She was stuck and you gave her a way out. You set her free. You truly did send her to a better place."

"It doesn't make what I did right," I say in a hoarse voice.

"No, it doesn't, but it helps you deal."

"Did you love her?"

He pulls back and stares down at me. "Only woman I ever loved."

"Why?"

He gives me a half smile, but it's pained. "She was nothin' like you described her. To me, she was Emily. Sweet, caring, loving, Emily. She didn't do horrible things. She loved you. Heck, she loved me. The woman you speak of, that wasn't the woman I got a glimpse of. Each time you talk about her, I lose a little part of the woman I remember."

159

"Am I hurting you?"

He grips my face. "You've been hurtin' me every fuckin' day since she took you, and now, you hurt me each day you look at me with those broken eyes. You hurt me, 'coz I wasn't there to fuckin' save you when you needed savin'."

"You didn't know," I rasp.

"Don't make it any easier."

"You're here now."

He nods and sucks in a deep breath. He stands. Clearly, the emotions of it are too much for him.

"Never told you this, Addi, 'coz I was too proud, but I should have told you the minute you broke into my compound and stepped into my shed."

I give a weak giggle.

"I should have told you that I love you, and I've loved you since the second I laid eyes on you. Ain't never changed, and it never fuckin' will."

Only a biker can use the word fuckin' in the same sentence as I love you, and make it sound breathtaking. I smile up at him, even though I'm still crying.

"You know, I think I might just love you too, old man."

He chokes a laugh and shakes his head. "'Nuff of this sappy shit. You're makin' a girl of me. You need me to get you something?"

I shake my head. "No, you're giving me enough."

He nods and then digs into his jeans pocket, he pulls out a fifty and thrusts it at me.

"What's that for?"

160

"Food, you know, bein' that I'm your dad and all that," he says, using the same line I used on him the first night I arrived.

I burst out laughing, and with a grin, he leaves me to it.

Well damn.

Who knew a group of bikers really could be my happy ending?

~*CHAPTER 17*~

PRESENT

"Cade, are you home?"

I hear the female voice as I'm cooking breakfast a week later. I've been staying at Cade's house the past few nights, because he decided not to go on the ride to find Jasper. Instead, he stayed behind to make sure I had protection in case he showed up. The Hell's Knights have been gone over three days, but so far, they haven't found anything. That bothers me more than I'm letting on. I drop the scraper I was using to flip eggs, and walk over to the front door. I see a young, beautiful woman standing behind the screen. She's absolutely stunning. She has this long, lightly curled blonde hair and eyes that remind me of cats eyes; they're yellow and completely out of this world. She smiles when she sees me approach, which makes me think she knows who I am.

"Hi, can I help you?" I smile, opening the screen.

"You must be Addi?"

I nod. "I am, and you are?"

"I've heard a lot about you, I'm Ciara."

This is Cheyenne's sister? My heart does a strange flip flop, perhaps in awe of how strong this girl must be to live through what she's lived through.

"Ciara, it's nice to meet you. Come in, I'll get Cade."

I turn and she follows me inside.

"So, are you enjoying being here?" she asks.

"I am. So far it's been good."

"And I hope Cade's treating you well?"

I laugh. "Yeah, he's doing a great job."

"For a biker anyway," she laughs.

I turn, giving her a grin. "Yeah, for a biker. Can I get you something to drink?"

"No, I'm okay, thank you."

"Ciara?"

I turn when I hear Cade's voice. He's coming down the stairs, looking like a dark angel, with his messy hair, light eyes and shirtless state. My heart speeds up, and I lick my lips.

"Cade, I hope you don't mind me stopping in?"

Cade grabs his shirt from the couch as he passes it, throwing it on. He breezes past me, putting a kiss to my lips before stopping in front of Ciara. He reaches for her, and pulls her into his arms. For some reason, his actions don't bother me at all. He's clearly got a good friendship with this girl, and I'm happy for him. Everyone should have a good friend.

"You know you can always stop in, what can I do for you, Tomcat?"

She grins and rolls her eyes at him. "You all know I hate that nickname?"

Cade smirks, and reaches out for my hand, pulling me close. "It's the eyes," he says.

"Damn eyes, I'll never live them down."

Cade chuckles. "Did you meet my girl?"

Ciara nods. "I did. She's lovely."

I grin at her, and she returns it. Then she turns back to Cade. "I'm here about Spike."

Cade flinches, and I rub my hand up and down his back, soothing him.

"What about him?"

"I know he's in town."

"He won't bother you. We've made sure of that."

"I kind of wanted to talk to him."

Cade raises his brows. "You can't be serious? Every time you two are in the same room, you end up ripping each other's fuckin' heads off."

Ciara rolls her eyes. "Don't be so dramatic; we only half tear them off."

Cade laughs and I find myself laughing too. Ciara has a bubbly personality. She's the kind of girl I could get along with quite easily. She's not much older than me either by the looks of it. Maybe twenty-three.

"Why would you wanna see him anyway?"

"I wanted to talk to him. Look, I know I was harsh on him. What happened wasn't anyone's fault. My sister made her choice; it wasn't Spike's fault it ended the way it did. I've had some time to understand that."

"Spike ain't gonna hear of it, you know that?"

She nods. "I have to try though. Maybe it will bring him some sort of peace. I know he loved Cheyenne."

"Your parents know you're here, Tomcat?"

Ciara visibly stiffens. "No, and it wouldn't go down well."

164

"You hated him for years after her death. You forgave me when it was my fault. He ain't goin' to take your apology well."

"It was no one's fault. Not yours or his. You were both trying to save her. It went wrong. It's the end of it."

"Ain't never that simple, and you know it."

She shrugs. "Sometimes it has to be."

"I don't talk to Spike, so you're gonna have to find him on your own."

"You know where he's staying through, right?"

Cade shakes his head. "You ain't goin' over there alone, Ciara."

"Don't get over protective with me, Cade. I'm not going to get hurt. He wouldn't hurt me."

"Spike's bitter."

"He's okay," I blurt and Cade turns, eyes widening. Shit, I have to fix that outburst. "I mean, he's not a monster, Cade. I've seen him a few times, and he's never tried to hurt me."

"He tried to hand you over to a pimp willing to kill you," Cade grunts.

"He didn't know."

"Still think it's a bad idea sendin' her over."

"Then we'll go with her."

Cade shakes his head. "A Hell's Knight can't go into a Heaven's Sinner's compound; it's far against the rules. We might have a truce to get along, but even that's out of bounds."

"Then I'll go with her."

"Like fuck," Cade grunts.

"No, look," Ciara says, putting her hands up, "I'll figure it out. Don't you two tangle yourselves up in it."

"You ain't goin' alone, Ciara."

She gives Cade a look. "I'm a big girl."

"No."

"Let me go with her. Spike won't hurt me, Cade, and you know he won't."

"I said, fuckin', no," he grates out.

Ciara puts up her hands. "Stop arguing you two, it's fine. I'll leave it for now, okay?"

Cade gives her a look, and I cross my arms.

"Spike won't hurt me Cade, what's the problem?" I protest.

"The problem," he grinds out. "Is not that I think Spike will hurt you, 'coz I know he won't. The problem is that it's Heaven's Sinner's territory now, and we don't fuckin' go on their territory. That includes you, Addison. I won't fuckin' tell you again. You're not fuckin' goin'."

God, I hate bossy Cade. I give him a glare, which he returns with full force.

"Whatever, I've got to go to work," I snap.

"I'll make a few calls," Cade says, though his voice is still hard. "Then I'll take you."

"I'm heading over to the compound," Ciara says. "I can take her."

I turn to her. "That would be great, I'd prefer your company right now. I'll just go and get changed."

Cade snorts, but I brush past him and head up the stairs. I walk into his room, and begin changing for work. A moment later he comes in behind me.

"The fuck was that about?"

I spin around, buttoning up my pants. "That was because you think you can control everything I do."

"It's not about control, it's about respect for another club."

"We only wanted to talk to him," I snap.

"Don't fuckin' care. You won't be goin' there, Addison. You got it?"

"Yeah, I got it!"

I storm past him, shoving his hand away when he reaches out to grip mine. I head downstairs, and out the front door. Ciara is waiting beside her car. She smiles when she sees me.

"Ready?" she asks.

"Yep, ready."

I don't look back at Cade's house as I slide into Ciara's front seat. When she pulls out of the drive, I turn to her.

"Head to Spike's."

Her eyes widen. "Addison, that's not a good idea. Cade said no."

"It will take five minutes, he won't know."

"Addison..."

"Trust me, Ciara. Do you want to speak to Spike or not?"

She nods weakly. "I do."

"Then go."

"Are you sure about this?"

"Fuck yes I'm sure, Cade doesn't own me."

"He kind of doe…"

"No," I growl. "He doesn't. Let's go."

We're both silent for long moments, then Ciara turns to me again.

"You honestly didn't have to do this, Cade will be furious."

"He'll get over it. It's about time Cade learned he can't tell me what to do."

"God girl, you've got far too much spunk."

I laugh. "So, you and Spike? Things seem pretty bad between you two."

She sighs and pulls a set of sunglasses over her eyes. "Yeah, it started long before my sister passed. Spike was my first, if you know what I mean?"

My mouth drops open. "Cade said you had a crush on him. He didn't say he slept with you!"

She laughs. "Cade leaves out those details. He's just protecting me."

"So you and Spike…have history?"

She shrugs. "I suppose you could call it history. We met one night and we became friends. I knew he was crushing on my sister, but I didn't care. I was a revenge fuck, I'm sure of it. He saw her one night out with another man and he got angry. He found me at the bar, and one thing lead to another. We had sex. He didn't know it was my first time until later when my sister went sick at him. She cared about him too, and was using the other man to make him jealous. When she found out Spike slept with me, she got angry. I

168

was heartbroken, being used like that. I knew Spike had feelings for me, but they weren't as strong as the ones he had for Cheyenne. I went away for a while. When I came back they were married."

Jesus, that's a fucked up story. I can't imagine how painful that would have been for Ciara, loving a man who was not interested in her at all.

"I'm sorry, that would have been awful," I say gently.

"It wasn't nice."

"Do you still care about him?"

She quickly glances out the window. "No," she says, but I can see how her body stiffens. Ciara is in love with Spike; it's written all over her.

"What's his real name?" I ask, changing the subject.

She giggles. "You know, I didn't know the answer to that until a few years ago."

I smile. "Everyone calls him Spike; he clearly has no need for his name."

"No, I suppose he doesn't. It's Danny."

I giggle loudly. "How did they get Spike out of Danny?"

She flushes and I give her an 'oh you have to tell' look.

"Oh spill!" I urge.

"Well, Spike is known for his…well, spikes."

"His spikes?"

"He has numerous, um, spikes in his…"

"Oh, Jesus!" I yell.

Ciara laughs. "He has to take every one of them out when he gets lucky, they're literally sharp spikes. There's about seven of them."

"What is wrong with that man?" I laugh. "He's got some seriously twisted fetishes."

She nods. "I've heard. The piercings are one thing, but putting big spikes in them, is a whole other story."

"It must get frustrating for him to have to take them out every time."

She flushes again. "He makes it part of the…experience."

"I'm sorry what?"

"He makes it a task for women, or at least I've heard that's what he does. He has them remove them, while they're…you know…sucking him."

"La la la la la!" I cry, pressing one hand to my ear. "Don't wanna know!"

Ciara laughs. "No one said the man was normal."

"Clearly, he's not normal," I chuckle.

Ciara and I chat the entire way to the old warehouse the Heaven's Sinners have decided to shack up at. We park the car outside the large gates, and slip out. Ciara looks nervous as we walk towards the gates, her hands are fumbling together over and over.

"It's going to be fine," I say, though I'm not sure it is. Even my heart is thudding now. I know it's a risk coming here, and I know if Cade finds out, I'm dead. God, me and my stubborn head.

"I hope so," she murmurs.

When we reach the gates, I rattle them loudly and call out, "SPIKE!"

Ciara stares at me, completely shocked. "Aren't you worried about screaming at the fence of a massive MC lot?"

170

"No."

I watch as a group of bikers walk out of the warehouse, guns in the air. Spike walks out behind them, looking as utterly breathtaking as he always does. I wave to him, giving him a grin. "It's me!" I yell in a singsong voice. I'm being sarcastic, of course, but I'm just trying to lighten the mood.

Ciara gapes at me. "Are you asking to get shot?"

"Spike won't shoot me. If he wanted to, he would have. Trust me," I murmur.

Spike waves his hand, and the men lower their guns. He pulls a pair of sunglasses over his head and begins walking towards us. When his gazes fall on Ciara, he stops. He just stops dead in his tracks.

"The fuck are you doin' here?" he barks at her.

"Play nice, Spike. She only wants to talk," I say.

He turns to glare at me. "What the fuck are you doin' here?"

"Visiting my old pal."

He raises his brows at me. "You got far too much sass, girl."

I grin at him. "Just admit it, you want to be my friend."

His lips twitch, and there's something about Spike that makes me feel completely safe around him. He's kind of like Cade; he acts tough, and I have no doubt he is, but he's also gentle inside. It's written all over him. For someone like me, that's lived a life around evil, I can pick the people that have black hearts and the ones who are just putting on a show.

"You're lucky your man paid me my money."

"You and I both know you never wanted to hurt me, Spike."

He raises his brows. "I'm reconsidering that decision."

171

I grin again, and watch as he turns back to Ciara. She's just watching him. I can't see her expression or his, because they're both wearing sunglasses.

"Why are you here, Ciara? Ain't got nothin' to fuckin' say to you."

His voice is hard, but I can hear a hint of pain behind his anger.

"I just wanted to talk with you."

"As I said," he growls, "ain't got nothin' to fuckin' say."

"If you'll just let me…"

"What part of that don't you understand?" he barks. "You're nothin' to me. You never were. You were no more than a revenge fuck. Stop tryin' to be my friend; it's too late for that. You let your folks drag me through hell to get vengeance for your sister. You made my life a living hell. I couldn't care less if you dropped off the face of this earth."

My mouth drops open, and Ciara nods weakly. "I understand. I do. I just wanted to say sorry. I wanted you to know I forgive you."

"Forgive me?" he roars, storming over and gripping the fence. He shakes it hard. "Forgive me for what? For tryin' to protect her? That other cunt is more to blame than me. I never wanted her to leave the fuckin' house. You forgave him right away, so don't you fuckin' come in here and try to make yourself feel better. That's all you're fuckin' doin', is makin' your own demons go away. Fuck you, Ciara."

Spike spins around, storming towards the warehouse.

"Spike, please, you know I care about you!" she calls, her voice raw and broken.

"Go and fuckin' die!" he roars, throwing the rude finger up over his shoulder. Well, that went well.

Ciara turns, rushing off towards the car. I just stand at the gate for a moment, before yelling, "Hey you!"

Spike stops and turns, looking at me. He's panting, his body trembling with rage and emotion.

"You're a fucking jerk! If I could get past this gate, I would kick your ass! I know you're better than that, Spike, it's written all over you. Stop living behind that shield, it's so fucking see through."

I don't give him a chance to respond. I turn on my heel and walk off towards the truck. When I get in, Ciara is crying. I reach across and grip her hands.

"He'll come around, just give him time."

God, I hope I'm right.

Because it's clear as day to me – Spike and Ciara have some

I arrive back at the compound an hour later for my shift. I know I'm late, but that's not uncommon for the girls that work there; it's about time I got my turn. When I arrive, Cade is pacing outside the front doors. Uh oh. He turns when he hears my boots crunching, and he comes storming over. I guess he figured out what I just did, either that or he's just pissed I went out and didn't tell him where. When he reaches me, I can see his eyes flaring. Shit, he's pissed.

"What. The. Fuck," he barks.

"What?" I say, in a casual tone.

"You fuckin' went behind my back, and took Ciara to the Heaven's Sinners lot."

God, he knows everything.

173

"She wanted to see Spike," I snap. "She had the right."

"I fuckin' gave you a direct, mother fuckin' order."

"You don't own me, Cade! We might be together, I might be your Old Lady, but you don't fucking own me!"

He's panting with rage now. "Do you have any fuckin' idea how bad that could have gone? Do you have any clue what those men could have done to you?"

"They weren't going to hurt me," I yell.

"Fuck it, Addison," he roars. "When are you goin' to fuckin' grow up?"

"Stop treating me like this," I cry. "You think you can just tell me what to do all the time, but you can't!"

"I fuckin' can, and I fuckin' will."

"No!"

He steps closer, gripping my shoulders. "I protect what's mine, you fuckin' know that. You runnin' off like that, you put yourself and me in danger. If you don't fuckin' care about yourself, fine, but you should fuckin' care about this club. What would you have done if Spike decided he didn't like you on his territory? What would you have done if he decided to start a fuckin' war? What if someone you loved got hurt, because of you? That could have happened far more easily than you could fuckin' imagine. Wake up to yourself, Addison, the world don't fuckin' revolve around you."

He lets me go, and storms away. My heart is thudding, and his words burn me to my very core.

Because they're true.

They're so horribly, painfully, true.

~*CHAPTER 18*~

PRESENT

"Order up!" I yell, sliding a tray of beer towards Mindy.

She spins, grips the tray and takes it to the group of bikers sitting on the table to the left of us. I begin pouring another lot of beers. I hear the rumble of Harley's coming into the compound, and I realize my father and the guys are back from their trip to find Jasper. I finish up with the beers, and walk out to greet them. When my father sees me, he puts a smile on his face, but it's fake. I can see right through him.

"You didn't find him, did you?" I say when I get close.

"No, we couldn't find him."

My chest tightens, but I force a smile. "It will be fine. He'll show up."

"He could be hiring anyone to find you now Spike has pulled out."

"Did you ever think of asking Spike to tell him where I am, and luring him close?"

"Thought of it, but it's too risky. If one of us isn't on our game, just for a second, he could have you."

"What are you going to do?"

"I'm goin' to talk to Spike."

"Why?"

"Because he can make contact, might be able to track the bastard."

175

"He will come out, Dad, you shouldn't be risking so much trying to find him."

Jackson gives me a sharp look. "The fucker raped my baby girl and made her life a living hell. I'm going to kill him, slowly. I'll put every waking minute into finding him."

"I don't want you to get hurt," I whisper, sounding far more vulnerable than I would like.

Jackson meets my gaze, and he gives me the best smile he can muster up. "If I died defending you, Addi, then I would die knowing I finally did what was right by you."

I nod, though my chest hurts after his words. Jackson leans down, brushing his lips across my head. I close my eyes and just let the moment sink in; it's a moment I've waited my entire life for. The moment, where everyone who should love you, does. When Jackson pulls back, I give him my best attempt at a smile, which isn't great, but it's something. And something is better than nothing, right?

He gives me one last smile, then disappears into the compound with the guys. I am just about to head in after them, but I see Cade standing at the door of his shed. He's still angry at me, and yes, I can see why. I deserve everything I got from him. I wave to him, but he simply turns and walks inside. Sighing, I stomp across the dirt until I reach the shed door. I step inside and see him fiddling with his bike. I don't honestly know what to say to make this better. A simple apology just won't do it.

"I fucked up," I begin, and he looks up from his bike. His green eyes meet mine. "You're right, I could have put everyone in danger. I was thinking of myself, and my determination to avoid being controlled. I don't have an excuse for that. I won't use my past, because I don't live in it anymore. I should have listened to you, but I didn't, for that I'm sorry."

His eyes narrow, but he doesn't say anything, so I continue.

"I've lived so long avoiding being controlled, that it's almost built into me. I want to be with you, Cade, but I don't want to be in a relationship where I don't get a say so in my own life."

"Picked the wrong fuckin' man then."

"Cade," I snap. "Don't...just listen..."

"I'm listening, sugar," he rasps. "I'm fuckin' listenin' to every word. I know what you're sayin'. I feel what you're sayin', but it doesn't mean I'm goin' to back down. I am what I am, and when it comes to protectin' you, I'll do what I have to fuckin' do, even if you don't like it. You gotta learn to trust that, or you'll just end up hatin' me."

He's right, I hate it, but I know he's right. Every time he's told me to back down, it's been for a damn good reason. I need to let go, or I'll end up hurt and without anybody to protect me.

"You're right, I do need to trust you, and I do. What I did, it was fucked up and wrong. It could have ended badly. I'm only lucky it didn't."

"You gonna start listenin' to me?"

I nod. "If you start being nicer about it."

"If I think you're makin' a mistake, I ain't gonna be fuckin' nice about it. Don't mean I don't care about you, 'coz I fuckin' do. The reason I do it, is 'coz the idea of losin' you, is somethin' I can't fuckin' live with."

And there it is. The words I so desperately needed to hear. I walk over, gripping his face. He grumbles as I bring my lips down over his. He reaches up, tangling his hands in my hair, and deepening the kiss. Our tongues slide against one another's, and my body aches for him. He presses against me, hard and aching, and I want him. I need him.

177

"I want you," I murmur against his lips.

"Take me then, baby," he growls.

I begin lowering to my knees, and his eyes grow hooded. He knows what I want. I know what I want, and so I'm just going to take it. I grip his belt, yanking it off before unbuttoning his jeans. His hard cock springs free as soon as I slide them down just a touch. He tangles his fingers into my hair again, and rasps, "Suck me, baby, hard."

God, yes! I lean forward, snaking my tongue out and sliding it across his head. He hisses and tugs my hair tighter, bringing my lips down over his cock. I wrap them around it, letting him slide into my warm depths. With a groan, he pulls his cock back out, and slides it in again, and again, and again.

"Fuck, sugar, so fuckin' good."

I whimper around him, and continue sucking hard and fast. My saliva lubricates him as the pace begins to quicken. I reach up, cupping his balls in my hand and rolling them, gently massaging.

"Fuck," he groans.

I gently squeeze the tight sack, and he growls loudly. My head bobs harder, faster, until my mouth is sliding up and down his length with perfect rhythm.

"Fuck, goin' to come, baby."

I feel his cock swell against my tongue, then he comes, hot and hard, deep into my throat. I take all of him, swallowing every last drop and relishing in his growls and hisses of pleasure. When he's gone soft, and he's completely content, I slip my mouth from him, and he pulls his jeans up before taking hold of my shoulders and bringing my body up so we're flush together. His lips graze my head, and he holds me close like that for a while. I can hear his heart thudding against my ear.

"Fuckin' hate fighting with you," he rasps. "But fuck, makin' up is worth every second."

I giggle.

So typical.

~*CHAPTER 19*~

PRESENT

"I didn't talk to the fuckin' pimp," Spike says, taking a deep puff of his cigarette.

Cade growls at him, and Jackson pulls him back.

"Don't play bullshit with me, Spike. You fuckin' did talk to him."

Spike smirks. "No, I didn't. I spoke to his minions, who relayed his messages to me."

"Then give us the fuckin' minions numbers," Cade snarls.

"Well," Spike chuckles. "All you had to do was ask, buddy."

The way he says it is so cold and emotionless. My heart hurts for these two men; it hurts because I know once they were so close. I wonder if Spike will ever forgive Cade? While the two are in different MC clubs, they all seem to have an unspoken truce between them. There's not a huge hatred between the clubs, like there is with most. Perhaps that's because there used to be such a bond, and deep down, neither of the guys truly want bad things to happen to the other.

"Don't fuckin' play with me, Spike."

I put my hand on Cade's arm, and he gives me a brief look. Spike watches the two of us for a moment, then he digs out his phone and rattles off a bunch of numbers. Cade takes note, then he turns to Jackson.

"Let's go."

"Thanks, Spike," Jackson says, his voice gruff.

Spike shakes his head and then turns, heading towards the gates. Usually a Heaven's Sinner wouldn't be allowed in the compound, but Jackson made an exception for my safety. When Cade begins heading inside, I tell him I'll just be a moment, then I turn and rush after Spike. He hears my boots crunching behind him, and I notice his shoulders tense up.

"What do you want, precious?"

I smile, completely enjoying the fact that he knew it was me even before I said anything. If Spike ever let me in, I imagine we could actually be good friends.

"Why are you such a jerk to him?"

He snorts, but keeps walking. I catch up, until I fall in step beside him. He looks at me from the corner of his eye.

"He deserves it."

"He didn't kill Cheyenne," I dare to say.

Spike's entire body stiffens, and he spins around, glaring down at me. "Don't say her fuckin' name. That name means jack shit to me now, and so does Cade."

"We both know that's not true. You're as broken as he is."

Spike lashes out, gripping my shoulder and hurling me up close. "Don't pretend to fuckin' know me. You'll never know what I feel. You have no fuckin' idea what pain is, girl."

"I do," I grate out between breaths. He's hurting me, his fingers are pressing so deeply into my skin it burns. "I know because I've lived through pain. I know because I've put hate in front of feelings, so I didn't have to deal with them. You're not a bad person, Spike, and neither is Cade. He made a mistake; he lives with that every day. He sees her face each time he sleeps. He made a bad call, but he

181

made it because he was trying to pull you out of a fucked up situation, that you put yourself in."

Spike's panting now, but his fingers ease up. "You're dancin' with the wrong wolves, girl. You don't know me and what I'm capable of. Right now, you're pushing my limits."

"Do you think I'm afraid of you? I'm not. I'm not because I see the good in your eyes, the same good I see in Cade's."

He lets my shoulder go, and his eyes burn into mine. "Do you ever fuckin' give up?"

I shake my head. "No."

"Why me? Can't you find someone else to try and make friends with?" he snaps.

"I could, but those people don't need it as much as you."

He grunts. "You have no fuckin' idea what you're talkin' about."

"Is that so? Then why aren't you hurting me like you've threatened to do so many times?"

I know it's a risk saying that, because he could very easily turn and give away my location because he wants to prove a point. His eyes flare, and his mouth forms a straight line, but something in his expression has softened just a touch.

"Don't make a habit of hurtin' girls," he says gruffly.

I smile. I can't help it. He narrows his eyes, clearly confused.

"You will admit you like me one day."

He grunts. "Not fuckin' likely."

I beam at him, because I can see the amusement behind his poor attempt at a glare. I spin around, pleased with myself. I begin walking back to the compound, but before I'm too far away, I call over my shoulder to him.

"See you around, buddy."

I don't see his expression, but I imagine it's one filled with confusion. Spike just needs to let his demons go. I wonder if Ciara will be the girl to do that for him? I hope so. She seems right for him. She's got a backbone hidden behind that sweet exterior, and one day, that backbone will cause her to snap at Spike. Maybe then, they'll make some decent progress. He feels something for her too, it was written all over his face the day we stopped by his warehouse. He's just not ready to admit it yet. It's coming though, and boy, will it come with a boom.

"Pleased with yourself, aren't you?"

I roll my eyes at the sound of Britney's voice. I turn and see her walking towards me, a snarky expression on her face.

"Do you ever give up?" I say, crossing my arms.

"You think you've got them all under your thumb. Little miss darkness comes in, making them all work for her affections. They'll get bored of you eventually."

I sigh. "Are we onto this again? Give up, you're no more than a good time to these guys. They use you, feed you and get rid of you. They do that because you let them. You put yourself in the situation where you gain no respect, because you don't keep your legs closed. Just face it, you'll never be anyone's Old Lady."

She scowls and steps up closer, and I get a whiff of her overpowered perfume. "You'll get what's coming to you, bitch."

I wave my hand and turn. "Heard it all before, move on."

I walk off, leaving her alone. I'm tired of her shit; the girl seriously needs to move on. I step around the side of the house, and head down to Cade's shed. I left my purse there earlier. When I get in, he's on the phone, cursing at some poor person on the other end. He notices me standing at the door, and tones down his excessive cussing. I walk in and take a seat at his old desk. I pick up a few mags and begin flicking through. My cheeks flush when I come across some seriously raunchy articles. One of them is oral sex positions. I tilt my head to the side and feel my eyes widen at the position the couple is in.

"Yeah, call me back with details."

Cade snaps his phone closed and walks over, stopping behind me. I hear his light chuckle when he realizes what it is I'm reading.

"Curious, baby?" he murmurs, tangling his fingers in my hair.

"I suppose you could say that, yeah. How the hell do they do that?"

"Stand up," he orders, removing his fingers from my locks.

I spin on the chair and stare at him. "What?"

"Stand up, I'll show you."

I grin at him. "No way."

"Baby, get the fuck up, and get over here."

"No way you're doing that to me."

"Gonna feel fuckin' amazing. Now get up."

"No."

He smirks and walks over, gripping my shoulders and pulling me up. He leans down close, brushing his lips across mine.

"Trust me, you're gonna want to try this. Now, get your pants off."

"Cade, you'll never hold me!"

He gives me an arched brow, and then he leans down and grips my shorts. "Off, now."

"Cade…"

"Sugar…"

"Yeah, I know," I grumble, shifting out of my shorts. "Shut the fuck up."

He laughs and turns, walking over to the shed door and locking it. Then he spins back towards me and grips his jeans, lowering them as he moves. God, why does he have to be so fucking yummy? When he reaches me, his jeans are lowered and his cock is out, hard and pulsing. My attempt at pretending this wasn't a good thing, is now turning into complete, desperate want. I stare down at his erection, and my tongue slides out and across my bottom lip.

"Want that, sugar?"

"You know I do," I purr.

"Then come here, get those panties off, and let's play."

I drop my panties without a second question. I stand before him, pussy exposed, ready for anything he's got to give. He steps forward grinning, and huskily murmurs, "Handstand, sugar."

I flush and bend down, putting my hands on the ground. Cade leans down, grips my ankles and lifts me, bringing my legs up. My belly is facing his belly, and my pussy is now right in front of his face. His cock stabs me a couple of times as he adjusts us, hooking my legs around the back of his neck until my ankles are locking. Then he wraps his arms around my midsection and brings me up higher until his mouth is hovering over my open, sensitive flesh. His cock is at my face now, throbbing, needy. I wrap my fingers around it, still feeling completely nervous that I'm upside down and wrapped around him, and we're about to go for one hell of a 69 job.

185

"I can fuckin' smell you. Fuck, you want me, sugar," Cade growls and I can feel his breath against my pussy.

"Stop talking," I mewl.

He chuckles, and leans his head down, grazing his tongue across my sensitive tissues. I groan and take his cock, feeding the head into my mouth. He grunts and the vibrations travel through my clit. I take him deeper, sliding him in and swirling my tongue around his head and over his piercings. At the same time, he sucks my clit into his mouth and flicks the end with his tongue. I open my mouth and gasp as pleasure shoots through my body. He jerks his hips, bringing my attention back to his cock. I close my lips over him again, and suck with everything I have. He returns the favor until we're a mass of moans and trembling legs.

"Fuck," Cade snarls, wrenching his lips from my sex. "Need to be in you, deep."

"Yes," I gasp. "God, yes. Fuck me."

He gently lowers me, and I reluctantly let go of his cock. I place my hands on the floor and when he lets my legs go, I lower them down. Panting, I get to my feet and turn to face him; we're both holding the same lusty expression. Cade lets his gaze travel the room, until he stops at a set of chains hanging from the roof.

"Go hold those chains baby, now."

I do as he asks, walking over and reaching up, wrapping my fingers around the chains. He comes up behind me, sliding my hair from my neck and leaning down to brush his lips across my skin, I shiver and tighten my hold around the chains. Using his feet, he kicks my legs apart. His hard body is pressing against my back, and fuck, it feels good. He runs a hand down one of my legs, sliding his lips down my back as he goes. He grips my ankle and lifts it, putting it on a nearby toolbox. Now that I'm open and exposed, he reaches around and swipes his finger through my arousal.

"So fuckin' ready for me."

"Fuck me naked," I whimper. "I got tested."

I didn't tell Cade, but I got myself tested for diseases. I didn't honestly know after Jasper, if I would have any or not. I want to feel Cade, all of him, so it was my only option. Luckily for me, I am clean. Jasper must have covered himself when he was with other girls; I can only thank God for that.

Cade stiffens behind me, and rasps, "The pill?"

"On it."

"Fuck."

He grips my hips, grinding his erection against my ass.

"Been fucked here, sugar?" he growls.

"No," I whimper, letting my head fall back and my hair tumble down my back.

"Won't fuck you in a shed if you haven't had it, that takes time."

He jerks his hips again, taking hold of his cock and sliding it up and down my slick heat.

"Ready for me, baby?"

"Yes," I cry out, desperately.

With a throaty chuckle, he slips the head of his cock into my entrance. I whimper and push my backside back, needing more. He grips my hips, steadying me while he continues to feed his length inside me, little by little. One of his hands is now pressed flat against my belly, and every now and then, he puts a little pressure on it and pushes my body back.

"Cade, just fuck me," I gasp.

He thrusts deep, filling me, stretching me. His hand slips from my belly to find my exposed clit and he gently strokes it as he pulls his cock out, and pushes it back in harder, faster.

"So fuckin' hot for me, baby. You feel so fuckin' good like this."

I groan and rasp, "Pull my hair."

"Fuck. My dirty girl."

He tangles his hand in my hair, and jerks my head back, pressing his lips to my exposed neck while he drives his cock in and out of my heat. My fingers are throbbing around the chains; I'm gripping them so tightly. I can feel his breath on my ear as he leans over me. It's so intense. I feel my body rising, needing my release so desperately. I'm so close; I can feel it pulsing through my body.

"Cade, oh God!" I cry out.

"Come for me, sugar," he growls.

I thrash, not releasing my fingers as I come hard around him. My mouth opens, and I scream. Yes, scream. Cade growls behind me, and thrusts harder, hand tangled in my hair, finger rubbing my clit. A moment later, he roars and I feel him pulsing deep and hard inside me. He thrusts his hips until every last drop has been wrung from his body. Then he slumps down, wraps his arms around my mid-section, and rests his mouth against my back.

"Fuck," he rasps.

"That about covers it," I whisper.

"Let go now, baby, I got you."

I let go of the chains, and collapse back into his arms. He holds me like that for a long moment, before pulling back and spinning me around. He grazes his lips across mine, then pushes my sweaty hair off my face. He strokes my cheeks, and runs a finger across my bottom lip.

"Saw you talkin' to Spike out there," he gruffly says.

"Spike's not so bad, Cade."

"Never said he was."

"He'll forgive you one day. I know he will."

"Maybe."

Cade's gruff voice tells me he doesn't want to talk about it any further, so I pull back and smile up at him.

"I should go and get some clothes, it's time for work," I frown.

Cade grins at me. "Tough life, eh?"

I giggle. "Yeah, tough."

"You want a lift?"

"No, I'll walk. I need some fresh air."

"Not fuckin' walkin', sugar, end of fuckin' story."

Well then.

"I'll ask around, see if anyone can take me then. Most of the girls are finishing their shifts now," I say.

He nods. "You do that, yeah? I gotta keep makin' some calls, but you come back if you can't get a lift, and I'll take you."

"Have you gotten closer to finding him?"

"Nah, seems the fucker is good at hiding."

"It'll come good; he'll stuff up somewhere."

Cade doesn't look so confident, but he forces a smile for me anyway. "Call me when you get back, yeah?"

189

"Got you. I'll see you later, okay?"

"Missin' something vital there, sugar," he chuckles, staring at my bare ass.

"Yeah," I laugh. "I was getting there."

I pull on my panties and shorts, and straighten my hair out. I lean over, kissing Cade once more before turning and leaving the shed. As I walk through the compound, I relish in the good feeling that's swelling in my chest and spreading through my body. I'm finally happy, and it fucking rocks. I know I should ask for a lift, but Jackson's house is close and it's on a main highway. It will be time wasted getting a lift, so I decide to walk. It will be fine.

I head out of the compound and begin walking down the road, enjoying the fresh air. All I can think about is Cade's body over mine. God, I can still smell him all over me. I don't hear the car stop behind me until its engine switches off. That's when I realize how heavily I was daydreaming. I spin around expecting to see Cade, but he's not who I see. Instead, I see Jasper. Everything in my body comes to an abrupt stop; I'm almost sure of it. I can no longer feel my heart beating, or my legs moving. I'm just standing in complete shock.

"Well, well, bet you didn't expect to see me?" he hisses.

Oh God. This isn't good. Jasper has a gun in his hand, and he twirls it in his fingers. If I make a move to get my phone, it's quite likely he'll shoot me.

"W-w-what do you want?" I say.

"You know what I want. I want revenge."

What can I say to that? Right now my words are stuck in my throat. I can't get them out, even if I try. They're just lodged in my throat, along with my heart.

190

"What's that? Nothing to say to me, snake? That's perfectly okay, because soon enough, you won't be speaking at all."

"Just leave me alone," I rasp.

He throws his head back and roars with laughter. "Leave you alone? Now you're just being funny. Get in the car."

"No," I whisper, trembling.

He points the gun at my groin, and I stiffen.

"Don't make me ruin all my plans by shooting you now. I have so much to do to you first. Get in the car, or I put a hole in you right now."

Oh God. My legs wobble as I walk toward the old van. Jasper follows me and presses the gun against my back. I close my eyes, praying someone comes past. Please don't let him take me again.

Jasper leans over me; I can smell his stale breath as he opens the back of the van. "Get in, and if you even try and get out, I'll scatter your brains over the road."

I climb in, my whole body fighting against me. If I don't get in, then I could likely die right now without giving Cade a chance to find me. I still have my phone. I can only hope I get a chance to use it before Jasper takes it away. Jasper steps back, slamming the back of the van, then he walks around to the front seat. If we weren't on a big, open road, I'd leap out and run, but I have no doubt Jasper would put a bullet in me if I tried that. When the van lurches forward, my stomach follows suit. I wrap my arms around myself, and pray for escape. I peer out the glass in the back wishing there was a way out.

As if my prayers are answered, I see Spike and his MC club members ride up over the rise behind us. I peer through the glass, and slowly put my hands up just enough that they can see me waving, but Jasper can't. Spike raises a hand, to indicate he's seen

191

me. Then he raises a gun. Oh no, that's not a good idea. If Jasper gets killed, he could roll this van at the speed he's going, and I'd very likely die, too. I wave my hands, shaking my head slightly. Spike lowers his gun, and speeds up, that's when Jasper notices them behind us.

"Who the fuck is that?" he roars.

"I don't know," I lie.

"Put your fuckin' hands up!"

I do as he asks, giving Spike my best 'please, just go get help' look. Jasper points the gun over the seat, and he aims it at me.

"Tell them to fuckin' back down!" he orders.

I shake my head at Spike, pleading with my eyes for him to turn away. Jasper speeds up the van, and my heart begins to race. Spike gets closer. I can see his eyes now, and it surprises me to see that he looks as though he's worried. I shake my head again, and he shakes his back, like he's not willing to back down.

"I'll fuckin' shoot you. Tell them to back the fuck down!" Jasper roars.

I put my hands together as if I'm begging, and mouth over and over. "Call Cade, please. Call Cade, please."

Spike looks torn. I can see it in his face. I am paying so much attention to him, that I don't even notice that the guns gone off, until I see blood splatter across the back of the van window. Then I feel the deep, burning pain ripping through my shoulder. I open my mouth and scream, and my body slumps forward. Jasper shot me. I vaguely see Spike slowing down. I guess seeing me get shot made him realize Jasper isn't playing. The bikes spin around in the middle of the road, and go full throttle in the opposite direction. I scream out in pain as my back hits the floor, sending the pain shooting further into my shoulder.

"You think I'm fucking joking, snake?" Jasper roars. "You'll die for what you did to me!"

My vision begins going fuzzy as the pain takes over, rushing through my body like liquid fire. I can't even hear my own screams anymore. I'm fading out.

"Shut up!" I hear Jasper roar. "Shut the fuck up."

I feel my eyes roll; it's all just too much. It hurts too much. I feel my lids flutter closed, before my entire world goes black.

I scream as Jasper hits me with the butt of his gun, again. He's been doing it over and over, constantly. His mission is to punish me, slowly, painfully. I wish to God I had just let him shoot me on the road. I should have at least tried to run. Now, I'm here, and quite likely going to suffer a long, slow death. I spit blood on the floor as my mouth fills with it yet again. My shoulder aches. At first, it was a burning, agonizing pain, but now it's a constant, thudding pain. I guess all the hits to my face directed the pain from my shoulder to my head.

"They'll kill you for this," I spit at Jasper, who's watching me. I can almost see the evil ideas spinning in his mind.

He laughs, deep and malicious. "Won't matter. I'll have my revenge."

"You're willing to give up your life, for revenge? How pathetic," I hiss.

"You want to know what pathetic is?" he growls. "This!"

He grips his pants, and jerks them down. I open my mouth and gasp at the sight of his mangled, purple, and scarred skin. There's no longer any man parts. Now, it somewhat resembles a burn victim's skin. My eyes widen at the damage I did, but I'm not sorry. I'll never be sorry.

"Do you know what you fucking did to me?" he roars. "You fucking ruined my life. I don't care if I'm fucking dead, so long as you go down with me."

"You deserved everything you got," I bark.

"And you deserve everything you're about to get."

He storms over, grips my hair and pulls it so hard bits of it come out. I scream and squirm in my binds. My scalp feels like it's one fire, as each tiny strand of hair is ripped from the skin.

"Stop!" I beg. "Please!"

"No! You'll scream until every last drop of blood leaves your body."

He lets go of my hair, spins around and twirls his gun. "Now, what shall we start with? I'm thinking a few bullet holes, then perhaps I'll make you pay slowly, and painfully. You think just because you removed my working parts, that I can't hurt you the way I used to?"

That doesn't sound good. My skin prickles, and my heart begins thudding so loudly I can't hear myself think.

"Let me go, you piece of shit!"

I'm desperate now, and I can hear it in my voice. Begging won't work for me though. I already know begging gets him going. It gets most sick people going; it's what spurs them to keep up the torture. God, why can't I just pass out? Why can't my body just know what's going to happen, and put me out of this misery.

He laughs again. I hate that sound. I hated it back then, but I hate it more now. "You thought you were so smart, blowing off my dick. You thought it would save someone from experiencing the same torture, but you were wrong. You only made me more determined.

See now, snake, I can make it painful. Considering you were so fond of being raped, I'm thinking we'll start with this…"

He reaches into the back of his pants, and pulls out a massive knife. The sick feeling that washes through me in that moment cannot be explained. My entire body goes numb. My eyes go fuzzy, and my ears begin to ring so loudly I can't hear anything else around me. He's going to rape me with a knife. He's going to rape me…oh, God. No. No. NO! I struggle in my binds again, nearly snapping my wrists. God, come on.

Jasper laughs loudly again. "Didn't think you'd like that idea. Keep struggling, snake, you know it only makes me want this more."

I'm panting now, close to hyperventilating. The ringing in my ears has now become a loud roar. I am still pulling at my binds, beyond desperate to get away from him. Nothing in this entire world could possibly frighten me more than the idea of being raped with a knife. That is something you don't recover from. That is something that destroys you.

"You destroyed me. I destroy you. Fair is fair. I could just blow off your sweet little cunt, but that would ruin my fun. I want to hear you scream. I want your blood on my hands," he growls, then he grins. "You know, it was one of your own that gave away your location?"

What is he talking about?

"What?" I rasp.

"Britney, is that her name? Yeah, she got word to me. Clever girl she is."

Oh, God, no…Britney did this? My whole body trembles. I knew she was capable of a lot of things, but this? She handed me to the wolves.

"Hurts when someone stabs you in the fuckin' back, doesn't it?" he snarls.

"Fuck you," I spit.

"Oh no snake, I'm going to fuck you."

He walks towards me running his fingers over the blade of the large knife. I squirm harder. I can't survive this. God, someone please help me. Tears leak out of the corners of my eyes, and they burn as they tumble down my cheeks. My own saliva is sliding down my chin; I am struggling to breathe so much I've forgotten how to swallow.

"Would you look at that. I think I've finally cracked you, snake."

He drops to his knees in front of me, and I try to kick out my legs at him. Growling, he drives the knife into one of my thighs. I scream. God, I scream so loudly he stumbles backwards and covers his ears.

"Shut the fuck up!" he roars.

Blood pours from the wound in my leg, and I begin to thrash. He lunges forward, holding the knife up to my face.

"You fuckin' move again, I'll slit your throat!"

I stop kicking, even though everything inside me is screaming at me to fight. I'm so scared; the only thing I can think about is living another moment. Jasper uses the knife to slice my pants off. I am crying heavily now, gasping and begging for him to stop. He runs the knife up my leg, drawing a tiny line of blood. I cry out, the sound is broken and strangled, like that of a wounded animal.

"I can't wait to slide this inside you, snake. I'm going to enjoy every second watching you suffer the way you made me suffer. I'm going to enjoy every scream that comes from your mouth."

He slides the knife up my panties, right in the middle of my sex. It's not quite enough to cut me, but it's enough to scare the life out of me. I thrash again; I won't let him do this. I'll let him stab every part of my body before he even gets close to doing what it is he plans. Suddenly, he leans back, running his fingers along the blade again, giving me a thoughtful expression.

"You know, it's funny really. I thought of so many ways I could play this out. I've spent weeks thinking of nothing else. I thought about just killing you, but that wouldn't have satisfied my need for revenge. No, it had to be epic. I liked the idea of shooting you right in the cunt, but that just wouldn't have completely satisfied me either. Then I remembered how much you loved being forced, and your wise little idea of blowing my dick off sparked my final decision. You thought I'd never rape you again, but you were so wrong, snake. I don't need my dick to rape you; all I need is something…well…like this hunting knife. Imagine what this will do to your insides? Imagine how this will feel lodged deep inside you. Imagine the pain as I twist it, slicing you to pieces. Nothing will satisfy me more, than to hear you beg. In fact, I think it's time to hear that begging."

I shake my head, and my body trembles with fear as he looms closer. He leans down, sliding the knife under my panties. I wail loudly and struggle once more. The pain is nothing anymore; it's nothing compared to the fear ripping through my body. I've never been so afraid in my life. I've never been so helpless, so unable to control what happens to me.

"Please," I scream. "Don't, please."

"That's it, snake. Beg."

I shake my head, forcing my mouth closed, even though all I want to do is continue begging him to stop.

"So pathetic, just like you always were. How about I make it easier for you? Because I'm such a nice person."

He reaches into his pocket, and pulls out a few pills. I clamp my mouth shut. No way in hell he's going to get me high for this. That will ruin any chance of escape I have. He leans forward, and grins, thoroughly pleased with himself. The sick bastard.

"Open wide."

I keep my mouth clamped shut. Growling, he lurches forward and slaps me hard. I cry out, and as I do, he thrusts his hand into my mouth, jamming the pills down my throat. I scream and gag, spitting as much as I can back up. The binds burn against my wrists as I tug, desperate to get away. Jasper picks up the gun with a growl, and aims it at my leg, before pressing the trigger. The ripping pain that tears through my thigh has me choking on the pills as I scream. My eyes roll, and my body jerks.

"Swallow them, or I'll shoot you again, snake," he roars.

I swallow as best I can, now desperately wanting the pills to make the pain go away. It feels like flames are travelling up my legs, slowly burning me. I scream and thrash, God, someone please help me. I don't want to die. Not after every breath I've fought for. Jasper kneels again, and shoves the knife towards my panties. No, please. I kick out, trying to hit him, maybe I can hurt him badly enough with a decent kick to the head or chest.

"Perhaps, I'll slice your nipples off first, really get the party started."

He reaches for my shirt, and I begin gagging again. My head is spinning, and my vision becomes hazy. I feel him lifting my shirt, and I'm powerless to stop him. I am so far beyond fight. I am just a puppet for him now, and he knows it. He reaches my bra, cutting it off with the knife. When he has my nipples exposed, he brings the blade down. I scream again, but it's pointless, I have nothing left. I'm in so much pain; my head is so fuzzy, I am unable to do anything but scream. The cold blade presses down over my skin, and I begin to feel the intense, excruciating burn as it cuts into my skin.

"Put the mother fuckin' knife down!"

Cade? Oh God. Cade? It can't be. I must be hallucinating. My eyes flutter as I try to focus on the room around me. I finally see Cade, coming closer, gun drawn. Jasper moves quickly, pressing the gun to my head before Cade can get close enough.

"I'll shoot her!" Jasper yells.

"You fuckin' breathe, and I'll blow your fuckin' brains out."

"Shoot him, Cade, so we can take him outside and teach the fucker a lesson," I hear another voice say, but I can't make out who it is.

"I'll shoot…" Jasper screams, his voice high pitched.

Before he has the chance to even finish what he was saying, Cade points his gun down to Jasper's leg and shoots. Jasper drops to the ground and rolls, screaming in pain. Cade turns to me, and rushes over, dropping to his knees. He rips off his shirt, using it to cover me. My eyes flutter closed as shock begins to set in.

"Addison, baby, wake up. Come on, don't close your eyes."

"Addison? Oh fuck, baby, keep your eyes open."

Jackson, they're both here.

"Sugar," Cade says again, stroking my cheeks, urging my eyes to open.

"Hurts," I wail loudly, feeling the drugs beginning to bring out my hysteria.

"I know, hush, I know."

"She's high." That's Spike's voice.

"We need to finish this fucker," Cade growls. "Addi baby, hey, I got you."

"Don't move her," Jackson says. "She might be hurt bad. We need to check."

199

Cade peers over at Jasper, who's trying to slide towards the door.

"Fuckin' move, I'll blow your brains all over that wall," Cade roars.

"Take care of him," I hear Spike growl. "I'll get her out."

"Baby, you're gonna be just fine. We're gonna get you out," Cade rasps, then he says to Spike. "You fuckin' take care of her. Whatever you got against me, it ain't her fault."

"I'd never fuckin' hurt her. Go finish that scum."

Cade grips my face, coating his hands in blood. "I'm gonna be back in less than five minutes. You hang in there, baby."

"I'm okay," I croak. "Kill him, Cade. Make it count."

He nods, and then Jackson strokes my face, his eyes red and glassy. Then they both turn, stand, and haul Jasper up, taking him outside. I can't begin to imagine what they're going to do. I don't care either. Spike kneels down in front of me, swiping a bloody piece of hair from my face.

"You sure do know how to get yourself noticed. If you wanted this kind of attention from me, you should have just asked."

He leans in, inspecting the wounds on my head. My stomach begins to turn violently as he begins to gently move me.

"Talk to me, precious. What hurts?"

"Everything," I croak.

"He shot you twice, God knows what else, and you've lost a lot of blood. Your body is working overtime to get those drugs out of your system. We're goin' to get you up slowly. You tell me if anything hurts too much."

I nod, and just as Spike's wrapping his arms around me, I hear Jasper's screams. They're the kind of screams you don't forget in a hurry. They're the screams of torture. I jerk and begin sobbing wildly, over reacting because of the drugs in my body. My stomach turns harder, and I know I'm going to be sick.

"Hey, hey, calm down."

"Sick," I rasp out.

"Shit."

Spike gently lets me go just in time. I drop forward and begin throwing up violently. I hear Spike mutter a few 'fucks' before he grips my hair and moves it off my clammy face. When I've stopped throwing up, he gently sits me back and focuses instead on undoing my hands. I can hear Jasper's screams turn into high pitched begging. I don't know what they're doing to him. I don't want to know. I hear the sound of a gun, and then everything goes quiet.

"It's all over, precious."

It's all over? Years and years of abuse, of torture, of mental pain, and it's over? It's really over? Spike pulls me into his arms when he's done with my binds, and stands, walking towards the door. Cade meets us at the entrance, covered in blood. I don't even want to know how he got that much blood on him. I croak out his name and he takes me from Spike's arms.

"Thanks, I appreciate it." I hear him say to Spike.

"Yeah," Spike says, his voice full of emotion. "Anytime."

Cade cradles me in his arms, and the familiar scent of him soothes something inside me.

"She's in a bad way," I hear him say.

"Get her to a hospital," Jackson says, his voice hoarse.

"What do we fuckin' tell them?"

"Tell them it ain't none of their fuckin' concern, and if they want to argue, by all means, argue."

Cade nods and walks us outside. When the sun hits my bruised and battered body, I wince. It's so bright. Too bright.

"It's okay. It's all goin' to be all right soon."

"Hurts," I croak again.

"I know, sugar. We'll get you better."

I close my eyes and listen as he shuffles around. Then he places me down onto the backseat of his truck. He covers me with a blanket, and gets in.

"You need us to deal with this?" I hear Spike ask.

By this, I assume they mean Jasper.

"Yeah, appreciate it."

Before I know it, the car has started. My eyes begin to flutter closed, a mixture of relief and the drugs. My legs are throbbing, my shoulder burns and my entire body feels broken, but I'm here. I'm alive and most of all...

I'm free.

~*EPILOGUE*~

"Fuckin' makin' me work extra hard," Cade grumbles and tosses a bag of food onto my eating tray.

I grin at him. "I'm an invalid. Someone has to feed me."

He grunts. "Your hands still work, yeah?"

I shrug.

"And your mouth."

I shrug again.

"Then you ain't a fuckin' invalid."

I pout at him and he grins, walks over and tangles his fingers in my hair.

"Can't fuckin' wait for you to come home."

"I know," I say, stretching. "Two weeks is too long."

"Fuckin' tellin' me, my dick hurts."

I giggle and grip his face, bringing him down for a kiss.

"You know, hospital sex is said to be good."

He chuckles against my lips. "Don't tempt me."

"I'm not tempting. I'm serious."

His eyes widen and he pulls back to meet my gaze. "You're all sore and fucked up."

I roll my eyes. "I don't need my leg and my shoulder to feel my man's cock inside me."

"Fuck, sugar, careful."

"Fuck me, nice and slow."

"Can't here. That old nurse will come in and bust my bare ass in the air."

"The bathroom is private."

"Sugar…"

"There's a chair in there. I could ride you gently."

"Fuck."

I shove his chest gently and get out of the bed. My body is feeling better and better with each day that passes. My leg still gives me a little pain but mostly, it's all ok. I hobble a little as I walk towards the bathroom, and Cade follows with no hesitation. When we get in, I close the door and lock it. Then I grip him, pushing him towards the large chair in the corner of the room. It's a chair I imagine people sit at while keeping an eye on someone in the shower. Cade drops his ass down onto the vinyl covering, and looks up at me, reminding me of a little boy on Christmas with the expression he's giving me. It's that of pure excitement.

"Ready for this? We have to be quick."

He snorts. "Ain't gonna be long, baby, I can assure you."

I lift my hospital gown and drop my panties, and then I reach over and grip Cade's jeans. He's already bulging against them. Licking my lips, I release his cock. When the warmth of him fills my palms, I groan. God, I've missed him. I climb over his lap, and straddle him.

"Do I get a kiss before I get fucked?"

He grins, grips my hair, and brings my lips down over his. He kisses me deeply while he gently lowers me over his hard length. I whimper into his mouth as he fills me, causing little stings of pain to shoot through my body. The pleasure far outweighs the pain though, and so I keep sliding down. When he's inside me, filling me, I begin a gentle rocking motion. I tear my lips away from Cade's mouth, nestle my face into his neck, and breathe him in. His hands go around my waist, and he supports me, helping me lift up and down. I go easily, sliding over his length.

"Fuck, baby, not gonna last long. Missed your sweet pussy."

"Me either," I whisper. I close my eyes and bite his neck.

"Fuck, harder, baby."

I bite him harder and he growls, erupting inside me. At the feel of his pulsing, and the sounds of his groaning, I come hard. I clench around him and cry out into his shoulder as quietly as possible, as my much needed release rips through me. We rock like that for long moments, just enjoying the feeling of being so close, so together. I lift my head from his shoulder and look him right in the eye. "Well, now we can say we've done it all," I smile.

He grins and wraps his arms around me. "There'll be plenty more for us to discover, now you're free."

Being free is so completely overwhelming. I never imagined this was the path my life would take, but I'm certainly grateful it did. Now Cade and I can start creating something worth fighting for. Speaking of, I have noticed he and Spike don't seem as tense. I really hope they can find it in themselves to forgive and forget.

"You and Spike seem to be getting along better," I mention casually, but my heart is thudding with curiosity.

"Yeah, he even sat down and had a beer with Jackson and I the other night."

"I hope one day you two can sort it out."

He nods, grinning at me. "Yeah, sugar, me too."

"Did Jackson deal with Britney?"

When Jackson and Cade found out Britney was the one to give away my location, they were furious. I was too; she nearly had me killed, and for what? The chance to be someone's Old Lady. I guess it goes to show how desperate some people can become.

"He threatened her within an inch of her life. If she wasn't a girl, she'd be dead."

I have no doubt about that. I am still in mild shock over the fact that she would do something so low. Britney is very lucky she's alive right now, and I know she wouldn't dare show her face on the compound again.

"Did he order her out of town?" I ask.

Cade nods. "Fuck yeah, and she wouldn't dare come back."

I sigh deeply, relieved. "Well, at least it's all over now."

He nods. "Sugar, much as I love ya, it's kinda gettin' a bit slippery in there, if you know what I mean."

I laugh and lift myself off him. We both straighten ourselves up and head back out. I walk over to the large window, take a seat and stare out at the hills I can see over the tops of the hospital. That's the good thing about being on the top floor. Cade kneels in front of me, reaches up and takes my hands.

"Fuckin' love you, sugar. You know that, yeah?"

I nod. "Cade, I know that. I've known that for a while now. The thing is-"

"I want you to know how much."

Stubborn man is cutting me off at the one moment I want to tell him I love him.

"I know how much, the thing is-"

"Sugar, you're fuckin' changin' everything I am."

"You're changing everything I am too, that's why I wanted to-"

"Sugar, fuck," he growls. "Do you ever stop talkin' for five minutes?"

"I'm trying to-"

"Sugar!" he says, tugging my hands. "Shut the fuck up!"

"Why?" I cry.

"Because I'm tryin' to fuckin' ask you to marry me."

My entire world stops. I feel like I've been punched in the chest, but in the best possible way. He wants to marry me? Cade Duke – big, bad biker – wants to marry me? I feel my eyes burn with unshed tears, as a feeling of pure joy rushes through my body.

"That got your attention," he grumbles, then he squeezes my hands harder. "If you let me talk, you would let me say that you fuckin' changed me. I have never loved anyone in my life, but you, fuck…you changed that. I'm not goin' to get all sappy on you, 'coz we both know I don't do that shit, but I will tell you this, you're the fuckin' meaning of breathing for me. You're the reason I get out of bed each day and fuck, if that's love, I am gonna hang onto it and never let it go. So, will you marry me?"

I am crying now, but I laugh through my tears. "If you let me talk," I rasp. "You would have let me tell you that I love you too, you stupid, stubborn-ass biker!"

He stares at me, then he roars with laughter and pulls me into his arms.

"Fuck, sugar, here you go makin' me the happiest man alive."

"I won't tell anyone you said that," I choke between tears.

He chuckles again, and pulls back. He reaches into his jeans pocket, and pulls out a ring, no box, just a ring. Who needs a box anyway; real beauty should never be covered. Cade grips my hand, sliding it onto my finger. Perfect fit. I meet his gaze, and for a long moment, we just lock eyes. Happy. Content. That's what we are right now. He picked up my pieces and put me back together, even when I thought no glue would hold. Turns out Cade was my glue, and in a sense, I think I am his.

"Well, sugar," he murmurs. "You sure made it difficult to save you, but you know, I got there in the end."

I smile, and nestle in closer to him. "You know why? I didn't want to be saved before, but with you, that all changed. For once, I wanted to see what was on the other side."

"And was it worth steppin' over the line?"

I pull back, grip his face, press my lips down over his and kiss deeply. He responds, kissing me with everything he has. When he pulls back, I tangle both my hands into his hair and say, "Oh, hell yeah!" And I mean it, with every part that is me.

I mean it because the battle with Cade has changed my world.

I mean it because fighting to find love was so much more rewarding than fighting to survive.

I mean it because my whole world was in tatters, but little by little, Cade has helped me put it back together again.

Finally, I believed that I was good enough to be saved.

And who knew he would be the one to save me.

That's life for you – you never know which way it's going to go – you just have to trust it.

~*THE END*~

I know you all want more Addi & Cade, I promise you'll see more of them in the next books. Jackson & Spike will both have a story to tell, so keep an eye out.

Spike's story, Heaven's Sinners, will be released 25 th September 2013.

Made in the USA
Lexington, KY
31 March 2014